JEFF MACNELLY

the Shoe® must go on

An Owl Book
HOLT, RINEHART AND WINSTON New York

Published by Holt, Rinehart and Winston,
383 Madison Avenue, New York, New York 10017.
Published simultaneously in Canada by Holt, Rinehart and
Winston of Canada, Limited.

Library of Congress Catalog Card Number: 84-81352
ISBN: 0-03-000737-2

First Edition

Printed in the United States of America

1 3 5 7 9 10 8 6 4 2

ISBN 0-03-000737-2

ACT I
The First Act
Primus Actus
le Premier Acte
ACT ONE
Acto Uno

IT'S SENATOR BELFRY FOR YOU, SHOE.
HEE HEE... HE'S PROBABLY HONKED OFF AT YESTERDAY'S EDITORIAL...
SHOE? I JUST WANTED TO TELL YOU THAT I AGREE WITH YOUR GREAT EDITORIAL– 100 PERCENT!!
IN THAT CASE, I'LL RUN A RETRACTION.
MACNELLY

THESE COMPUTERS ARE TRICKY DEVILS.
THEY REQUIRE DELICATE PRECISION ADJUSTMENTS.
HAND ME THAT TIRE IRON...
MACNELLY

WHAT'S THIS CALLED?
WE CALL IT "TYPEWRITER."
ANOTHER FIELD TRIP FROM THE JOURNALISM SCHOOL, I SEE.
MACNELLY

WE OF THE TREETOPS HISTORICAL RESTORATION SOCIETY WOULD LIKE YOUR SUPPORT IN RESTORING THE DOWNTOWN AREA TO ITS ORIGINAL APPEARANCE...
SURE... SOUNDS OKAY TO ME — WHAT WAS IT LIKE ORIGINALLY?
MOSTLY TREES.
MACNELLY

AWRIGHT, BUDDY!! THAT'S ENOUGH FOR YOU! I'M CUTTIN' YOU OFF!!
AFTER ONLY TWO BEERS?
AND FIVE BOWLS OF PRETZELS...
MACNELLY

Y'KNOW MY UNCLE WHO LOST HIS JOB ON THE ASSEMBLY LINE TO ONE OF THOSE INDUSTRIAL ROBOTS?...
WELL, HE JUST GOT ANOTHER JOB ON AN ASSEMBLY LINE...
MAKING CARS AGAIN?
NO, BUILDING INDUSTRIAL ROBOTS.
MACNELLY

UNCLE COSMO!
AW, SKYLER, COME ON!
HOW CAN SOMEONE WHO CAN'T BALANCE A CHECKBOOK...
BE EXPECTED TO ORGANIZE HIS SOCK DRAWER?
MACNELLY

COMPUTER DOWN AGAIN?
YEAH... I'M SORRY I HAD TO CALL YOU OVER AGAIN, IRV...
I JUST DON'T UNDERSTAND THESE THINGS!!
WELL, LET'S START BY TRYING TO GET YOUR FIST OUT OF THE SCREEN...
MACNELLY

I WONDER HOW I'D LOOK WITH A MUSTACHE...
WHY DON'T YOU RUN A TEST?
HOW DO I DO THAT?
HERE...
CHOMP DOWN ON YOUR HAIRBRUSH.
MACNELLY

OKAY... BARTENDER QUIZ:
WHAT DO YOU GET WHEN YOU BLEND 2 OZ. OF SCOTCH, 2 OZ. OF CREME DE MENTHE AND A SCOOP OF COFFEE ICE CREAM?
A HANGOVER THAT REGISTERS 6.5 ON THE RICHTER SCALE.
MACNELLY

LET'S SEE.... I'VE GOT THE SHIN PADS, THE ARM PADS, THE CHEST PROTECTOR...
THE ARMORED GLOVES, THE MASK... THE HEAVY DUTY STICK...
GOOD GRIEF! IT'S NOT ENOUGH.
MACNELLY

THE SECRET OF GOOD GOAL-TENDING IS CROUCHING DOWN... MOVING OUT OF THE BOX TO CUT DOWN THE ANGLE...
AND WHEN THE SHOT IS FIRED...
MAKE YOURSELF AS SMALL AS POSSIBLE...
VOOM
MACNELLY

MUFFY?... I'D LIKE TO TALK TO YOU ABOUT YOUR LUNCH HOURS...
SURE.
I MEAN THE ONES YOU TOOK LAST FRIDAY.
MACNELLY

UNCLE COSMO?... I BOUGHT YOU A SURPRISE...
YOUR OWN PERSONALIZED LICENSE PLATE.
I'M DEEPLY TOUCHED.
WIDE LOAD
MACNELLY

THE PERFESSER AND SHOE ARE NEGOTIATING A NEW CONTRACT...
ARE THEY CLOSE TO AN AGREEMENT?
YEAH, IT'S JUST A MATTER OF DOLLARS AND CENTS.
$
¢
MACNELLY

IT'S TIME WE STOPPED GETTING PUSHED AROUND!!... IT'S TIME WE STOOD UP FOR OUR RIGHTS!!
WHAT ARE WE... CHICKEN?
OF COURSE WE ARE...

THIS IS THE LATEST IN MODERN EGG FARMING TECHNOLOGY...
AUTOMATIC FEEDING, AUTOMATIC SORTING, PACKING — EVERYTHING IS FULLY AUTOMATED...
EXCEPT, OF COURSE, FOR THE EGG-LAYING MECHANISM ITSELF.

YOUR COAT, SIR!
YOUR CIGAR...
LIGHT, SIR?
YOUR CAR, SIR.
WHO WAS THAT, UNCLE COSMO?
MUST BE A PUBLIC SERVANT.

AS I APPROACH MIDDLE AGE...
I'M DEVELOPING A BAD PROBLEM:
MY SHIRTS AND I TAPER IN DIFFERENT DIRECTIONS...
MACNELLY

WELL, LET'S SEE WHAT'S AILING THIS COMPUTER...
WHAM WHAM WHAM WHAM WHAM WHAM WHAM WHAM
WHAT WAS THAT FOR?...
TO GET ITS ATTENTION.
MACNELLY

Dear Mr. Furslinger:
I'm sorry it has taken me so long in getting back to you...
I did enjoy your thoughts about my column...
in which I urged Mr. Truman not to run for re-election.
MACNELLY

Y'KNOW, MUFFY... YOU'RE THE ONLY BILINGUAL JOURNALIST I KNOW...
YOU THINK IN ENGLISH...
AND TYPE IN SERBO-CROATIAN.
MACNELLY

UNCLE COSMO?... WE'RE GONNA SPEND THIS WEEKEND IN A REALLY UNIQUE WAY...
HOW'S THAT, SKYLER?
I HID THE TV SET.
MACNELLY

DELI
TAKE A NUMBER
62
62
FOUR!
MACNELLY

WHO'S THAT?
YOT.
HIS NAME IS YOT?
THAT'S WHAT I CALL HIM...
IT'S SHORT FOR "YOU OVER THERE."

#?!! LOST AGAIN!!
BEEP BEEP
WHAT'S THE SCORE?
WORD PROCESSOR-17,930 ...PERFESSER — ZIP.

AWRIGHT, MEN... ON DEFENSE, WHEN YOUR MAN PULLS UP FOR A JUMP SHOT KEEP THOSE HANDS UP!... RIGHT IN HIS FACE!!
OR IN YOUR CASE, SKYLER...
IN HIS BELLY BUTTON!

THE GREAT THING ABOUT MY TEAM IS THEY'RE ALWAYS BEHIND ME...
ESPECIALLY ON JUMP BALLS.
MACNELLY

I'VE GOT A BAD CASE OF COMPUTER CRAMP.
WHAT'S THAT?
IT'S JUST LIKE WRITER'S CRAMP...
BUT IN THE SEAT.
MACNELLY

GEE, PERFESSER, WHAT'S YOUR SECRET OF LONG LIFE?
SKYLER... IF I HAD KNOWN I WOULD LAST THIS LONG.
I WOULD'VE TAKEN BETTER CARE OF MYSELF.
MACNELLY

BOY, IT'S NICE AND TOASTY IN HERE.
YEAH, I GOT THE STOVE GOING.
YOU HEAT WITH WOOD?
NO, JUNK MAIL.
MACNELLY

AHA! A TASTY FISH DOWN THERE IN THE LAKE!! AND HE'S NOT MOVING!
HE'S JUST SITTING THERE! ...JUST LIKE HE'S FROZEN IN—
CLACK
THE ICE.
MACNELLY

HEY!! FAR OUT, MAN!! I HAVEN'T PLAYED THIS ONE YET!!
BINK
WHAT'S IT CALLED?
WASHING MACHINE.
MACNELLY

HEY, MRS. ZOOWICKY, HOW DID YOU GET TO BE A SCHOOL BUS DRIVER?
WELL, SKYLER, I USED TO DRIVE A TRUCK.
AND I MOON-LIGHTED AS A ZOOKEEPER...
SO I FIGURED, WHY NOT COMBINE THE TWO CAREERS?
MACNELLY

YOU USED TO DRIVE A TRUCK, MRS ZOOWICKY?
THAT'S RIGHT... I USED TO HAUL CHICKENS DOWN IN TEXAS.
GEE, THAT MUST'VE BEEN ROUGH WORK.
YEAH, BUT AT LEAST BACK THEN I DIDN'T HAVE TO RIDE IN THE SAME CAGE WITH THE BIRDS.
MACNELLY

I'M OPPOSED TO FORCED BUSING OF KIDS TO SCHOOL.
RIGHT ON!
SCHOOL BUS
BUSING KIDS HOME... NOW THAT'S ANOTHER STORY.
MACNELLY

AND NOW THE MOST ESSENTIAL STEP IN ICE FISHING...
CUTTING THE FISHING HOLE?
NO...
THE COOLER HOLE.
MACNELLY

THIS IS A GREAT APARTMENT... SOFT LIGHTS, SQUISHY SOFA... STEREO... WET BAR.
ALL THIS PLACE NEEDS TO MAKE IT THE PERFECT BACHELOR PAD...
IS A WIFE TO KEEP IT CLEAN.
MACNELLY

GENTLEMEN... EACH OF YOU HAS BEEN GIVEN A PRESS KIT WHICH YOU WILL FIND USEFUL IN FOLLOWING ALONG IN MY LECTURE ON ECONOMIC POLICY...
WHAT'S IN THE PRESS KIT?
PAJAMAS.
MACNELLY

CAN I TRY ONE OF THOSE CIGARS, SHOE?
SURE.
PUFF PUFF PUFF GOOD GRIEF!! THIS THING IS STINGIN' MY EYEBALLS!!
ANYBODY KNOWS YOU NEVER SMOKE A CIGAR WITH YOUR BASEBALL HAT ON!
MACNELLY

WHAT A BEAUTIFUL DAY FOR A FLIGHT...
BOINK
@☆#?!! PICTURE WINDOWS.
MACNELLY

WHY DO WE HAVE TO KNOW ABOUT ALL THESE FOODS THAT CAUSE CANCER IN RATS?
WHAT GOOD IS THAT?...
WELL, WE KNOW WHAT TO FEED TO THE RATS.
MACNELLY

I HOPE YOU'RE NOT DRIVING HOME TONIGHT.
NOPE...NOT IN MY CONDITION.
THERE ARE PLENTY OF OTHER, SAFER WAYS FOR ME TO GET HOME.
WHAP
FLYING, HOWEVER, IS NOT ONE.
MACNELLY

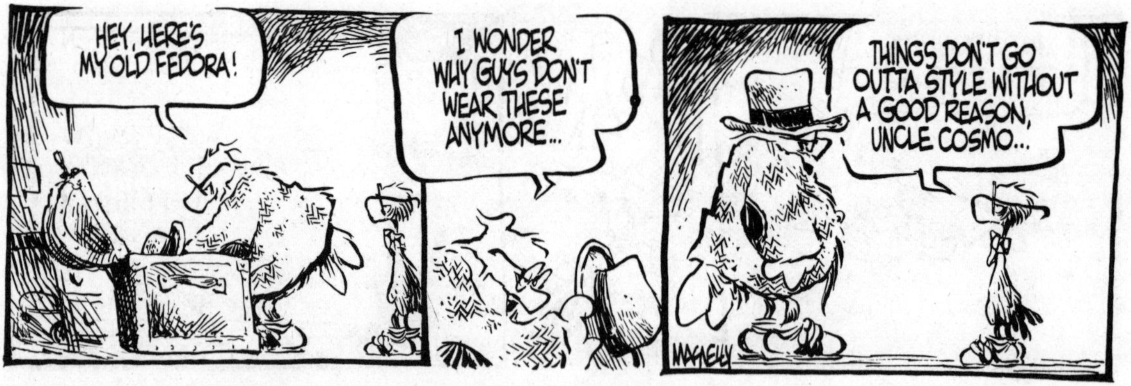
HEY, HERE'S MY OLD FEDORA!
I WONDER WHY GUYS DON'T WEAR THESE ANYMORE...
THINGS DON'T GO OUTTA STYLE WITHOUT A GOOD REASON, UNCLE COSMO...
MACNELLY

COULD I HAVE THE CLASSIFIEDS?
SURE...
YOU LOOKING FOR A JOB?
NO. JUST A BEDSPREAD.
MACNELLY

DO YOU GUYS KNOW WHAT YOU'RE DOING?
OF COURSE.
TREETOP'S VOL. FIRE DEPT.
WE'VE BEEN IN BUSINESS SEVEN YEARS...
AND HAVEN'T LOST A FOUNDATION YET.
MACNELLY

WATCH OUT, MRS. ZOOWICKY!
BEEP BEEP!
BUS
SCREECH!
DOO DOO HEAD!!
YOU'VE BEEN DRIVING A SCHOOL BUS TOO LONG, ZOOWICKY...
MACNELLY

IRVING, YOU'VE GOT TO FIX THIS G★#?! COMPUTER.
CALM DOWN. I BROUGHT THE JUMPER CABLES.
ZAP
WHAT IS IT?
I DON'T KNOW, BUT WHATEVER IT IS, IT'S HIGHLY CONTAGIOUS.
MACNELLY

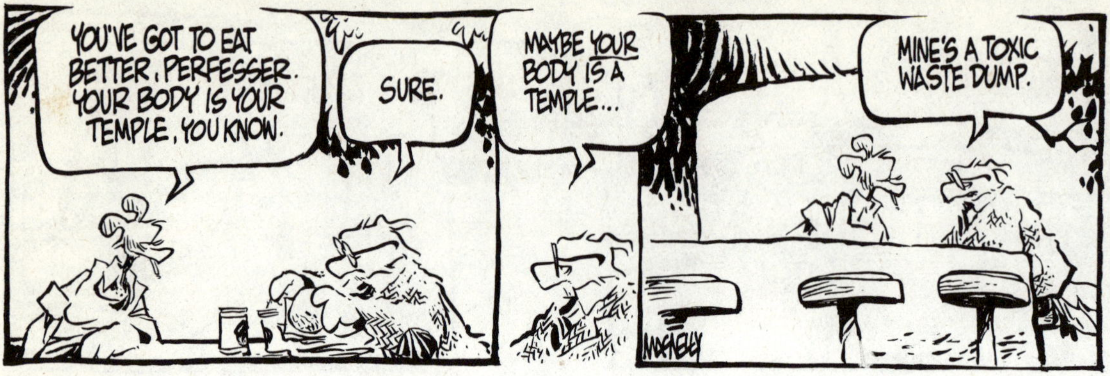
YOU'VE GOT TO EAT BETTER, PERFESSER. YOUR BODY IS YOUR TEMPLE, YOU KNOW.
SURE.
MAYBE YOUR BODY IS A TEMPLE...
MINE'S A TOXIC WASTE DUMP.
MACNELLY

I THINK I'LL TAKE SOME WORK HOME WITH ME TONIGHT...
UNCLE COSMO?
URMF?
WOULDN'T IT BE EASIER TO BRING YOUR HOME TO WORK WITH YOU?
MACNELLY

PERFESSER! YOU'RE STICKING TO YOUR DIET!
IT'S EASY.
I FOLLOW THE FIRST RULE OF SUCCESSFUL DIETING...
"NEVER LET ANYONE SEE YOU EAT."
MACNELLY

THEY FINALLY FOUND A FOOD THAT DOESN'T CAUSE CANCER IN RATS...
GREAT NEWS!
NOT REALLY.
THE FOOD IS LIVER.
MACNELLY

ROZ... WITH ALL THESE AVAILABLE MEN AROUND, WHY AREN'T YOU MARRIED?
BECAUSE I'M NOT INTO MOTHERHOOD, MASOCHISM OR MISSIONARY WORK.
MACNELLY

WANNA SEE THE WANT ADS?
NAH... THERE'S NOTHING IN THERE FOR A GUY WITH MY YEARS OF EXPERIENCE.
EXPERIENCE AT WHAT?
READING WANT ADS.
MACNELLY

SNAP! CRACKLE! POP!
DOES YOUR CEREAL TALK, UNCLE COSMO?
SURE.
THUD! CRUNGLE! POOMP!
GRANOLA.
MACNELLY

UNCLE COSMO!... WHY ARE YOU ALWAYS WATCHING MR. ROGERS' NEIGHBORHOOD?
BECAUSE MR. ROGERS LIKES ME JUST THE WAY I AM...
MACNELLY

ARE YOU GOING TO THE ROCK CONCERT TONIGHT, LOON?
NAH... I HATE CONCERTS.
BUT ROCK CONCERTS ARE DIFFERENT, LOON! YOU LIE OUT ON A BLANKET WITH A BOTTLE OF WINE AND EXPERIENCE!! YOU'LL LOVE IT!
THIS IS GONNA TAKE MORE WINE THAN I FIGURED.
MACNELLY

I'D LIKE TO PLACE AN AD IN SUNDAY'S PAPER.
YES...
HELP WANTED
WHAT WOULD YOU LIKE TO SAY?
"HELP."
MACNELLY

I'M GETTING REAL TIRED OF THE SNIDE STUFF THEY'VE BEEN HANGING ON THE NEWSROOM BULLETIN BOARD.
I KNOW, BUT IT'S GREAT FOR THE ESPRIT DE CORPS OF THE STAFF...
THAT BULLETIN BOARD IS A PLACE WHERE THE REPORTERS CAN JOSH THE EDITORS... HAVE A LITTLE FUN... YOU KNOW...
I KNOW.... MORALE MUST BE AT AN ALL-TIME HIGH IN THIS OUTFIT...
EDITOR
MACNELLY

WANT ANY MORE?
NO THANKS.
I'M JUST GONNA FEED IT TO THE DOG.
WELL, OKAY...
I HATE TO SEE SMALL ANIMALS SUFFER.
MACNELLY

WELL, I HOPE I'LL BE SEEING YOU THIS SUNDAY, SHOE...
REALLY?...
YOU GOIN' TO THE TRACK TOO, PADRE?
MACNELLY

I JUST GOT THE NEW FEDERAL REGULATIONS GOVERNING THE TRASH AND JUNK INDUSTRY...
WHAT A PAIN!!
NO... THESE REGULATIONS WILL ACTUALLY HELP BUSINESS.
JUNK
HOW'S THAT?
DO YOU KNOW HOW MUCH I CAN GET FOR HIGH-QUALITY SCRAP PAPER THESE DAYS.?
REGS
MACNELLY

WE'RE FROM EPA, MR. FISHHAWK... ABOUT THE TOXIC WASTE DUMP NEAR YOUR HOME...
WILL YOU HAVE TO EVACUATE ME?
NO, SIR...
WE THOUGHT IT WOULD BE EASIER TO MOVE THE DUMP.
MACNELLY

WHAT'S FOR DINNER, UNCLE COSMO?
I WAS GONNA COOK THIS FROM THE FREEZER...
BUT IT'S BEEN AROUND SO LONG, I DON'T THINK WE SHOULD EAT IT.
IT'S SORT OF A FAMILY HEIRLOOM.
MACNELLY

HEY, LOOK! GLOM FRUIT FROM SAMOA... 3¢ A POUND!
3¢
WHAT THE HECK DO WE DO WITH THESE UGLY BOOGERS?
LOOK, AT 3¢ A POUND WE COME OUT AHEAD IF WE JUST USE 'EM TO LINE THE DRIVEWAY.
MACNELLY

YOUR OFFICE IS A DISGRACE!! DON'T YOU HAVE ANY PRIDE?
SURE, I DO...
I HAVE PLENTY OF PRIDE...
I'M REAL PROUD OF THE SHEER VOLUME OF STUFF I'VE MANAGED TO CRAM INTO THIS TINY DESK.
MACNELLY

THIS PENTAGON BUDGET STORY OF YOURS IS WAY TOO COMPLICATED...
WRITE IT SO OUR READERS WILL BE ABLE TO UNDERSTAND.
Caspar has 223 billion apples...

CAN YOU FIX THIS THING, IRV?
NO PROBLEM — JUST HAVE TO REPLACE A PART.
WHICH PART?
THE BIG PART ON THE OTHER END OF THIS CORD.

HERE'S SOME LUNCHMEAT FOR YOUR SANDWICH, SKYLER...
LUNCHMEAT?
YUK! THAT SOUNDS SO UNAPPETIZING.
DOES "CHOPPED, PRESSED PORK LIPS" SOUND ANY BETTER?

THAT WAS MY STOCKBROKER, BILLIE SOL WRIGHTOFF...
HE'S GOT ME INTO A HOT NEW GROWTH STOCK...
A CHAIN OF MOLE REMOVAL CLINICS.
MACNELLY

I JUST REALIZED SOMETHING...
I'M THE TOUGHEST KID ON MY BLOCK.
EASY FOR YOU TO SAY, SKYLER...
MACNELLY

LOOK, PERFESSER, YOU CAN'T SOLVE YOUR PROBLEMS BY JUST DRINKING BEER...
YOU'RE RIGHT, ROZ.
MAKE IT A WILD TURKEY ON THE ROCKS...
MACNELLY

WHAT ARE YOU GOING TO DO THIS SUMMER, SKYLER?
I DON'T KNOW... HANG AROUND, GET A JOB, MAYBE...
UNLESS I GET DRAFTED...
AND GO TO SUMMER CAMP.
MACNELLY

HEY, MAN,...WHAT'RE YOU TUNED IN TO?...
IT'S NOT TUNED INTO ANYTHING.
THEN WHAT'RE YOU LISTENING TO?
UP UNTIL NOW, TOTAL SILENCE.
MACNELLY

DINNER WILL BE READY IN A FEW MINUTES....CHECK THAT MICROWAVE COOKBOOK AND SEE HOW LONG IT'LL TAKE TO DEFROST...
HOW LONG HAS IT BEEN FROZEN?
MICROWAVE
I DON'T KNOW... COUPLA YEARS, I GUESS.
THAT'LL TAKE 4.3 DAYS.
MICROWAVE
MACNELLY

DOES DRINKING EVER REALLY SOLVE ANYTHING?
SURE. I HAVE A PROBLEM THAT MY DRINKING ALWAYS HELPS.
WHAT'S THAT?
I KEEP WAKING UP IN THE MORNING STONE SOBER.
MACNELLY

IT'S OUTRAGEOUS!! I SPEND ALL THIS TIME WRITING MY COLUMN AND BLIPPO!!....
IT'S WIPED OUT WHEN I TRY TO FEED IT INTO THE MEMORY BANK!!.... YOU CALL THAT PROGRESS?!
YOU CALL THAT WRITING?
MACNELLY

DON'T THINK OF IT AS INCOME TAX — THINK OF IT AS A USER FEE.
RIGHT...
YOU USE ME...
THEN YOU CHARGE A FEE.
IRS
IRS
MACNELLY

Book Report: Moby Dick by Herman Melville
For one of the all-time classics of literature...
this is a surprisingly good book.
MACNELLY

Moby Dick is the story of one man's obsession with finishing off a mysterious, huge, white whale.
– something this reviewer can really identify with.
MOBY DICK
MACNELLY

YOU BETTER GET A JOB THIS SUMMER, SKYLER.... YOU'RE NOT GONNA HANG AROUND THE HOUSE ALL THE TIME WITH YOUR FACE GLUED TO THE TUBE.... IS THAT UNDERSTOOD?...
YESSIR.
NOW, GO HOME AND FINISH YOUR HOMEWORK. WE'VE GOT WORK TO DO.
MACNELLY

ANOTHER BEER, MAN MOUNTAIN?
SURE, ROZ, THANKS...
BOY, THIS JOGGING REALLY TAKES IT OUT OF YOU.
A FEW BREWS HELP MAKE A PHYSICAL FITNESS PROGRAM BEARABLE.
WELL, I BETTER START THINKING ABOUT TAKING OFF...
GOSH, IT'S ALMOST MIDNIGHT!!
SEE YA, ROZ...
I DON'T WANT TO TURN INTO A PUMPKIN...
OH NO!
TOO LATE!
MACNELLY

WE'LL HAVE A DOUBLE ORDER OF EGG ROLL...
TWO EGGLOW!
WON TON SOUP...
WAHTAZOOP...
SZECHUAN CHICKEN... AM I PRONOUNCING THAT RIGHT?
YES... SZECHWAH SHICKA...
MOO GOO GAI PAN?...
YES... MOOGA GUYPAH...
CHICKEN CHOW MEIN...
SHICKA CHOWMAY.
AND BRING US SOME CHOPSTICKS...
THANK YOU, SIR!
ISN'T THIS GREAT ATMOSPHERE? WE COULD ALMOST BE IN OLD CHINA...
GIMME A FORTY-TWO !! A THIRTEEN, A FIFTY-FIVE!! SLURP ONE AND THE E-ROLL TWICE!!
MACNELLY

GOOD GRIEF! HOW AM I GONNA GET MY PAPER?
HEY... WHY NOT FLY?
I'LL JUST ZOOM OUT OVER THE SNOW...
AND TOUCH DOWN TO RETRIEVE MY PAPER...
WITH THE DAINTINESS OF A HUMMINGBIRD...
CRACK
VOOMP
—A 200-POUND HUMMINGBIRD.
MACNELLY

GOALIE IS THE LONELIEST POSITION IN ALL OF HOCKEY.
BUT HE'S ALSO THE KINGPIN—THE ANCHORMAN OF THE TEAM.
THE GAME IS WON OR LOST ON HOW THE GOALIE PERFORMS.
HE CARRIES A HUGE RESPONSIBILITY FOR THE SUCCESS OF THE TEAM.
UH OH... THE WING IS COMING IN WITH THE PUCK ON A FAST BREAK!! NOW IT'S JUST HIM AGAINST ME!!
A CLASSIC DUEL! EYEBALL TO EYEBALL ON THE FROZEN BATTLEGROUND!!
IT'S ALL UP TO THE GOALIE NOW!!
FROOP!
WHERE WAS THE @★#?!! DEFENSE?!
MACNELLY

HURRY UP WITH THAT COLUMN!!
RIGHT! ...ALMOST FINISHED...
A FEW MORE CORRECTIONS ON THE WORD PROCESSOR...
AND NOW TO ENTER IT INTO THE MEMORY...
GLORP!
WHAT'S WRONG?
I'M HAVING SOME ELECTRONIC PROBLEMS...
WHAT'S THE MATTER WITH THE COMPUTER?
IT THREW UP.
MACNELLY.

WELCOME TO THE FABULOUS '80s, SKYLER!!
MEET OUR NEW HOME COMPUTER.
COMPUTER? WHY DO WE NEED A COMPUTER?
IT'S A FANTASTIC TOOL.
FOR ONE THING, IT HELPS WITH MY HOUSEHOLD BUDGET.
I'VE FED IN ALL MY EXPENSES, MY DEPOSITS, MY CHECKS, MY INVESTMENTS...
AND THE COMPUTER MAKES THE DECISIONS ON HOW TO MANAGE MY MONEY, SEE?...
WHAT'S IT SAYING?
"SELL THE HOME COMPUTER."
MACNELLY

HEY, CUT IT OUT, LENNY!!
HEY! LENNY STOLE MY LUNCH!!
LENNY!! DID YOU THROW MY MATH WORKBOOK OUT THE WINDOW?!
#*@?!
SCHOOL BUS
WUMP
HEY!!
WHOA!!
SCHOOL BUS
GOOD GRIEF, MRS. ZOOWICKY!! YOU WERE DOING ALMOST 40 WHEN YOU HIT THAT POTHOLE!!
...LENNY ALMOST BASHED HIS HEAD ON THE ROOF!!
REALLY?
THEN TOMORROW WE'LL TRY IT AT 45.
SCHOOL BUS
MACNELLY

I'D LIKE TO FIND OUT ABOUT STARTING AN INDIVIDUAL RETIREMENT ACCOUNT WITH YOU.
YES, SIR! WE HAVE A SPECIAL ON NEW IRA ACCOUNTS.
WITH A MINIMUM INITIAL DEPOSIT OF $2500...
YOU GET MAXIMUM MONEY MARKET RATES COMPOUNDED SEMI-HOURLY, ACCUMULATING TAX FREE, OF COURSE...
PLUS FREE CHECKING, LIFETIME SAFE-DEPOSIT BOX AT HALF PRICE...
LIFE INSURANCE, A TOASTER, A SET OF EIGHT GLASSES, A DIGITAL GRANDFATHER CLOCK AND A GALLON OF CHOCOLATE CHIP ICE MILK.
SOUNDS LIKE A GREAT DEAL...
ANYTHING ELSE YOU'D LIKE TO KNOW?
YEAH.
CAN I BORROW 2500 BUCKS?
MACNELLY

SHOE®
HEY, BARN BEAK!! CAN'TCHA READ?!!
EXPRESS CHECK-OUT 9 ITEMS OR LESS
YOU GOT TEN THINGS THERE...
YOU GOT TORTILLA CHIPS, BEAN DIP, MARSHMALLOW FLUFF, FISH STICKS AND SIX CANS OF BEER!!
LOOK, LADY... THIS IS A SIX-PACK...
IT COUNTS AS ONE ITEM.
NO, SIR! SIX BEERS, I COUNT SIX BEERS, AND THAT MAKES OVER NINE ITEMS!!
OKAY.
POIT!
GLORB
CRINK
EXPRESS CHECK-OUT 9 ITEMS OR LESS
MACNELLY

SHOE®
WE WANT TO DO THIS TOXIC WASTE DUMP STORY FROM EVERY POSSIBLE ANGLE.
LOON, YOU COVER THE E.P.A. ANGLE—WHAT IT'S LIKE TO TRY AND POLICE A DUMP...
—YOU'RE THE ONLY ONE WHO COULD EVER GRASP THE INS AND OUTS OF POLLUTION AND CLEAN-UP REGULATIONS...
I'LL COVER THE INDUSTRY ANGLE—WHAT IT'S LIKE TO WORK IN A DUMP.
MUFFY: HUMAN INTEREST ANGLE—WHAT IT'S LIKE TO LIVE NEAR A DUMP.
WHAT ABOUT ME?
YOU WRITE WHAT IT'S LIKE TO BE A DUMP....
MACNELLY

SHOE®
BIK
FOUR IRON, SKYLER...
TWINK
UH, THE FIVE IRON, PLEASE.
PLISH
SIX!!
DINK
7 IRON, PLEASE!!
PLINK
THE EIGHT IRON, PLEASE SKYLER....
18
BLIK
OKAY, NOW GIMME THE @☆#?!! PITCHING WEDGE!!
18
BWEE
FLIK
MACNELLY

SHOE®
I REALLY ENJOY MY SUNDAY MORNINGS.
THERE'S TIME TO SETTLE DOWN WITH A CUP OF COFFEE AND THE PAPER...
IT'S THE ONLY TIME OF THE WEEK WHEN WE HAVE A CHANCE TO RELAX AND THINK...
AND RECHARGE THE MENTAL BATTERIES.
IT'S A SPECIAL TIME TO CONTEMPLATE THE GREAT PROBLEMS AND PHILOSOPHICAL QUESTIONS OF THESE TROUBLED TIMES.
SKYLER ....MAYBE THIS IS A GOOD TIME TO HELP YOU DEAL WITH ANYTHING THAT MIGHT BE PUZZLING YOU.
DO YOU HAVE ANY DEEP PHILOSOPHICAL QUESTIONS THAT YOU ARE TRYING TO DEAL WITH ?
SURE.
WHY AREN'T THERE ANY BALD EVANGELISTS?...
MACNELLY

SHOE®
WHAT'S ALL THAT STUFF, BUMPKINS?
IT'S MY GARDENING EQUIPMENT, SKYLER.
GARDENING IS AN ANCIENT TRADITION WITH US BRITONS...
IT'S IN OUR BLOOD. WE HAVE A PASSION FOR GROWING THINGS.
SPRINGTIME ALWAYS FINDS THE ENGLISHMAN MUCKING ABOUT IN HIS GARDEN...
WHEREVER WE CAN FIND A SMALL PLOT OF MOIST, DARK, RICH EARTH...
THAT'S WHERE WE LOVE TO BE THIS TIME OF YEAR... STARTING A SEEDLING, PLANTING A ROW OF VEGGIES...
SETTING OUT THESE BULBS...
BUT WHERE ARE YOU GONNA FIND A PLOT OF MOIST, DARK, RICH SOIL AROUND HERE?...
IN YOUR UNCLE'S SOCKS DRAWER.
MACNELLY

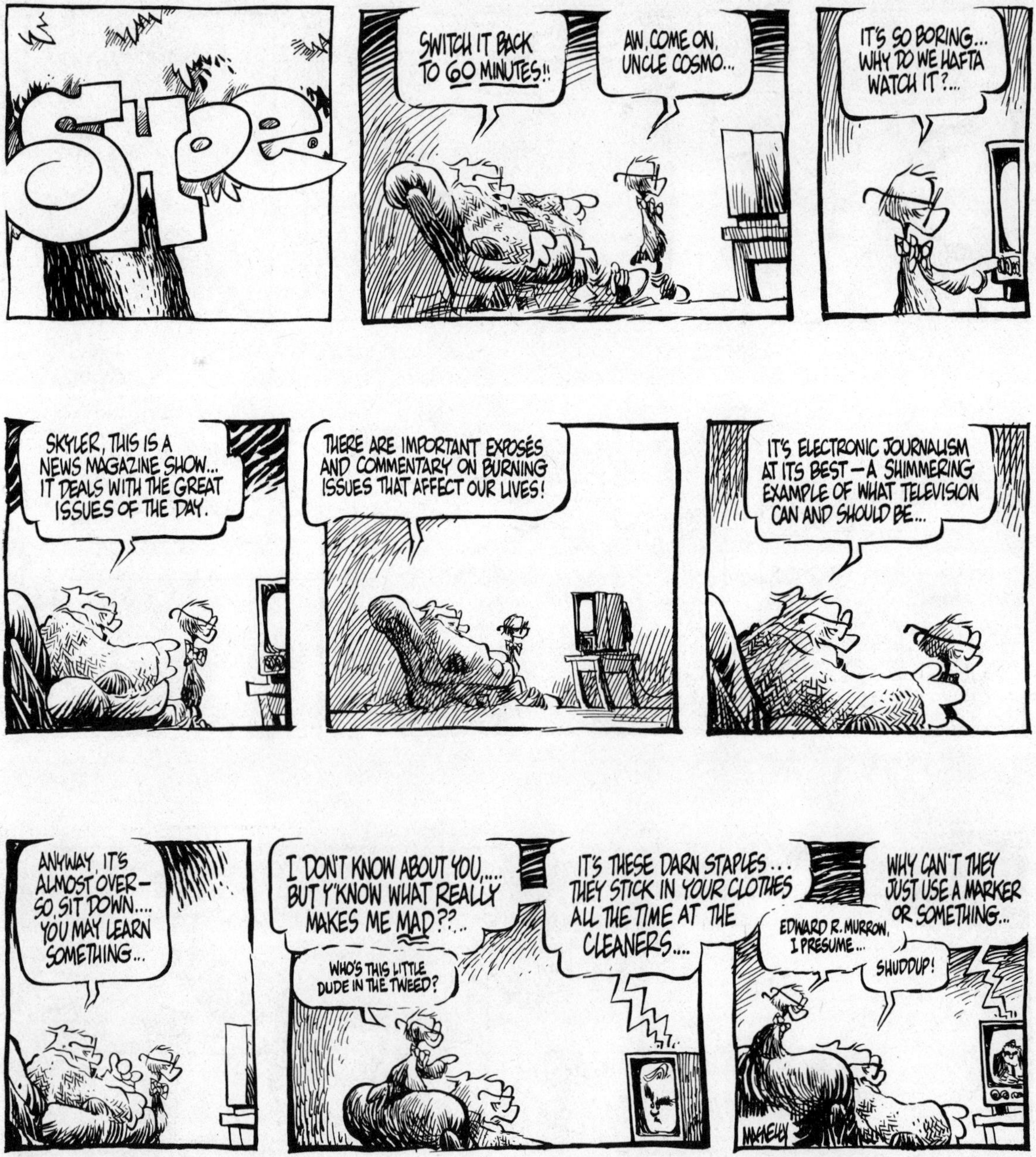
SHOE®
SWITCH IT BACK TO 60 MINUTES!!
AW, COME ON, UNCLE COSMO...
IT'S SO BORING... WHY DO WE HAFTA WATCH IT?...
SKYLER, THIS IS A NEWS MAGAZINE SHOW... IT DEALS WITH THE GREAT ISSUES OF THE DAY.
THERE ARE IMPORTANT EXPOSÉS AND COMMENTARY ON BURNING ISSUES THAT AFFECT OUR LIVES!
IT'S ELECTRONIC JOURNALISM AT ITS BEST—A SHIMMERING EXAMPLE OF WHAT TELEVISION CAN AND SHOULD BE...
ANYWAY, IT'S ALMOST OVER—SO, SIT DOWN.... YOU MAY LEARN SOMETHING...
I DON'T KNOW ABOUT YOU,.... BUT Y'KNOW WHAT REALLY MAKES ME MAD??...
WHO'S THIS LITTLE DUDE IN THE TWEED?
IT'S THESE DARN STAPLES... THEY STICK IN YOUR CLOTHES ALL THE TIME AT THE CLEANERS....
WHY CAN'T THEY JUST USE A MARKER OR SOMETHING...
EDWARD R. MURROW, I PRESUME...
SHUDDUP!
MACNELLY

SHOE®
Breakfast al Fresco - another recipe from the bachelor chef:
Take a standard-size bowl ...
Chip out the petrified Jell-O...
Select a box of your favorite cereal - break off a hunk.
crumble it into the bowl.
Take two teaspoons of sugar...
add to bowl ...
Select spoon and clean it thoroughly with thumb.
Pour on milk. (sniff first)
Bon appétit!
MACNELLY

SHOE®
MR. SHOEMAKER,... I NEED TO TALK TO SENATOR BELFRY ABOUT THIS STORY I'M WORKING ON...
BUT I CAN'T GET HIM ON THE PHONE – HE NEVER RETURNS MY CALLS...
MUFFY,... A GOOD REPORTER HAS TO KNOW HOW TO WORK THE PHONE.
LEAVE THIS ONE TO ME.
LEMME SPEAK TO SENATOR BELFRY.
I'M SORRY, THE SENATOR IS IN A VERY IMPORTANT MEETING.
WOULD YOU LIKE TO LEAVE A MESSAGE?
YEAH.
THIS IS THE WILD WEASEL MASSAGE PARLOR.... WE FOUND HIS SOCKS.
UH, I THINK I HEAR SENATOR BELFRY COMING OUT NOW...
MACNELLY

Act II

MUFFY,... IT'S ALMOST THREE O'CLOCK! WHERE HAVE YOU BEEN?...
I WENT OUT TO LUNCH WITH THE SENATOR.
HEY, YOU CAN'T HAVE A POLITICIAN BUYING YOU ANYTHING. THAT'S A CONFLICT OF INTEREST AND A VIOLATION OF OUR CODE OF ETHICS.
NO PROBLEM, MR. SHOEMAKER...
I CHARGED IT TO THE PAPER.
EDITOR
MACNELLY

PERFESSER?... I'M THINKING OF GETTING ONE OF THOSE DESKTOP COMPUTERS.
YEAH, THOSE ARE GREAT TO HAVE, MUFFY... I GOT ONE MYSELF...
IT'S SMALL, BUT IT DOES EVERYTHING - IT FILES INFORMATION, KEEPS MY CALENDAR, BALANCES MY CHECKBOOK - IT HAS ORGANIZED MY LIFE.... I'LL SHOW IT TO YOU...
IT'S IN HERE SOMEWHERE...
MACNELLY

ALL YOU EVER DO THESE DAYS IS SIT THERE STARING INTO YOUR BEER LISTENING TO COUNTRY MUSIC...
DON'T YOU HAVE ANY AMBITION LEFT?
SINCE YOOOVE GAWNNN
SURE I DO.
AN' LEF' ME BLOOOO HOOO
SOMEDAY I WANT TO CATCH THE GUY WHO KEEPS DOING ALL THOSE BAD THINGS TO CRYSTAL GAYLE.
DON'T SLA-AM THE DO- -OR...
MACNELLY.

WHY, SKYLER,... YOU BROUGHT HOME YOUR ALGEBRA BOOK...
I GUESS YOU WANT TO START YOUR LIBRARY ... AND IT'S A GOOD IDEA TO START WITH YOUR OLD TEXTBOOKS...
I KNOW IT'S FUN TO HANG ON TO YOUR BOOKS FROM THESE CHERISHED SCHOOL DAYS.
ALSO WE COULD USE A NEW THIRD BASE...
MACNELLY

Y'KNOW, SKYLER... I LOVE QUIET SUMMER EVENINGS, SITTING OUTSIDE,... RELAXED AND PEACEFUL...
I'M GOING TO PRESERVE THIS MAGIC MOMENT FOR THE WHOLE SUMMER...
HOW?
I'M SENDING YOU TO CAMP...
MACNELLY

UNCLE COSMO,... I'M PACKING FOR CAMP, BUT I CAN'T FIT MY CLOTHES IN THE TRUNK.
WHAT?
WHAT HAVE YOU PUT IN THERE?
JUST MY SURVIVAL GEAR.
MY STEREO, MY ATARI, 32 CARTRIDGES, THE APPLE II, FOUR CASES OF DR. PEPPER, MY BILLY JOEL ALBUMS...
MACNELLY

OH, COME ON, SKYLER... I KNOW YOU HAD A ROUGH TIME LAST SUMMER AT CAMP LEJEUNE.
BUT YOU GOT A LOT OUT OF IT.... BESIDES, IT'S A CHALLENGE!
HOW COME THE WORDS "CHALLENGE" AND "FUN" NEVER SHOW UP IN THE SAME SENTENCE?
MACNELLY
WELL, HERE YOU GO,... OFF TO GOOD OLD CAMP LEJEUNE.
YOU'LL HAVE A GREAT TIME, SKYLER....
IS THAT THE CAMP BUS?
YEAH... THE ONE WITH THE HURRICANE FENCE WINDOWS.
MACNELLY
GEE, THIS IS THE PITS.... THESE KIDS ALL LOOK LIKE THE GUYS FROM LAST YEAR... THEY GRUNT A LOT, AND THEY'RE SORTA SHINY...
CAMP LEJEUNE
BUT I DON'T SEE ANYONE I REMEMBER FROM LAST SUMMER.
HELLO, MAGGOT!
UH,... GOOD MORNING, SERGEANT!
MACNELLY

AWRIGHT, MAGGOTS, ... WE'RE GONNA SING THE CAMP SONG!! ...
OH, BROTHER.
YES SIR!!
YOU DO KNOW THE CAMP LEJEUNE SONG, DON'T YOU, MAGGOTS?
WHAT CAMP SONG?
YESSIR!!
FROM THE HALLS OF MONTEZOO-OOMA
LOUDER, MAGGOTS, LOUDER!!
I WAS HOPING FOR "MICHAEL, ROW THE BOAT ASHORE."
MACNELLY
AWRIGHT, YEW CLOWNS, FIRST ORDER OF BUSINESS!! PICK UP CAMP UNIFORMS!!
GREAT!! CAMP UNIFORMS! I HOPE WE GET SOME NICE SHORTS WITH STRIPES UP THE LEGS—MAYBE A CAMP SHIRT WITH A MONOGRAM, AND A BASEBALL HAT...
NEXT!!
BUT I KEEP FORGETTING: CAMP LEJEUNE IS NOT YOUR STANDARD SUMMER CAMP.
MACNELLY
I COULDN'T EVEN RUN A HALF MILE BEFORE I CAME TO CAMP LEJEUNE.
I GUESS YOU NEVER KNOW THE LIMITS OF YOUR PHYSICAL ENDURANCE...
UNTIL YOU'VE BEEN CHASED BY A DRILL INSTRUCTOR...
MACNELLY

GOSH, I'M HUNGRY...
NEXT!!
BLIT!
UH, WHAT IS THE MAIN COURSE?
GLOPH!
IT AIN'T STOUFFER'S LEAN CUISINE, CAMPERS!!
USMC
MACNELLY

WHAT A ROUGH DAY... WE'VE BEEN PAINTING THE BARRACKS SINCE BEFORE SUN-UP.
MESS
WE'VE GOT AN OLD SAYING HERE AT CAMP LEJEUNE:
IF IT MOVES, SALUTE IT; IF IT DOESN'T, PAINT IT;
BLIK
AND IF IT SMELLS FUNNY, EAT IT.
MACNELLY

OKAY... WHEN YOU MAGGOTS GET OUTTA CAMP LEJEUNE, YOU GOT A BIG CAREER DECISION TO MAKE!!...
INFANTRY.... TANKS,... HELICOPTERS,..... FIGHTERS... WHAT'S IT GONNA BE FOR YOU THERE, SNAKEBAIT?
ME?...
OH, I'M AIMING A LITTLE LOWER THAN THAT, SERGEANT...
I'D JUST LIKE TO GET TO THE SIXTH GRADE IN ONE PIECE.
MACNELLY

PITCHING FOR THE NEW YORK METS... TOM SEAVER!!
PRESS BOX
GO, TOM BAYBEEE!!!
HEY, SPORTSWRITERS CAN BE FANS TOO, YOU KNOW...
MACNELLY

I'LL NEVER UNDERSTAND WHY BASEBALL IS SO POPULAR. THIS GAME IS AS EXCITING AS WATCHING PAINT DRY.
COME ON, SHOE. BASEBALL IS WONDERFUL.
IT'S A GAME OF STRATEGY— OF STATISTICS.
THERE MUST BE A LOT OF ACCOUNTANTS WHO LIKE TO NAP IN THE SUN
MACNELLY

GAYLORD PERRY ON THE MOUND FOR THE METS – THE COUNT IS 2 AND 2...
HE'S AN INSPIRATION TO ALL OF US GUYS WHO LIMP INTO MIDDLE AGE.
HE PROVES THAT YOU CAN STILL COMPETE IF YOU'RE OVER 40...
SPLAT!!
STRIKE THREE!
YOU JUST HAVE TO HAVE A LITTLE EXTRA ON THE BALL.
MACNELLY

I CAN'T STAND TO WATCH THIS STUFF ON TELEVISION! THEY'RE GOING TOO FAR!!
ISN'T THERE ENOUGH GRAPHIC COVERAGE OF THE BASE ANIMALISTIC URGES OF MANKIND, WITHOUT SHOWING THIS STUFF?
WHAT STUFF?
ANOTHER BASEBALL MANAGER DROOLING TOBACCO JUICE.
MACNELLY

RINGGG!!!
HELLO.... STYLE SECTION.
MACNELLY

WE'VE GOT TO MAKE THIS PAPER MORE READABLE – MORE APPEALING TO THE AVERAGE READER.
HOW DO WE DO THAT?
RUN MORE PICTURES.
MACNELLY

Yesterday's windstorm caused no serious damage in the area,
but did manage to overturn a desk here at the Tattler Tribune.
Rescue workers are searching the rubble for survivors.
Editor
MACNELLY

ROZ'S ROOST
THE SEAFOOD HERE IS ALWAYS GOOD...
MENU
MENU
IT DOESN'T HAVE THAT FISHY TASTE.
MENU
MENU
MACNELLY.

WHAT AM I GONNA DO WITH YOU MAGGOTS?! YOU ARE A DISGRACE TO CAMP LEJEUNE!!
MAYBE I SHOULD WHUMP EACH ONE OF YOU LIZARDS WITH THIS M-1 RIFLE UNTIL YOU'RE JUST A QUIVERING PILE OF KHAKI-COLORED JELL-O!!
THAT WOULD SAVE THE MARINES A LOTTA TROUBLE!!
AND PUT YOU DISGUSTING MAGGOTS OUT OF YOUR MISERY!
THE SERGEANT'S SENSITIVITY TRAINING SEEMS TO BE WEARING OFF, I SEE.
MACNELLY

AWRIGHT, MAGGOTS... WE JUST GOT OUR ASSIGNMENT FOR OUR SUMMER CAMPING TRIP!!
GREAT! THE CAMPING TRIP!! IT'S ALWAYS THE HIGHLIGHT OF SUMMER CAMP.
NOW I'M PASSING OUT TO YOU IMPORTANT INFORMATION THAT YOU NEED TO KNOW FOR OUR TRIP...
WHITEWATER CANOEING IN CANADA, MAYBE?... HIKING IN MAINE?...
"POISONOUS SNAKES OF EL SALVADOR"....?
MACNELLY

AWRIGHT, MAGGOTS!! DOUBLE TIME!! TO THE OBSTACLE COURSE!!
WE'RE GOIN' TO THE OBSTACLE COURSE TO BUILD BODIES AND BUILD CHARACTER...
AND WE'RE GONNA BUILD MEN!, RIGHT, MAGGOTS?
YES, SIR!!
COULDN'T WE JUST GO TO SHOP AND BUILD BIRDHOUSES?
MACNELLY

COME ON, MOVE IT, MAGGOT! YOU GOTTA CROSS THIS RAVINE — AND ALL YOU GOT IS THIS ROPE.
WHAT DO YOU DO NOW, SON?
CALL THE ACROPHOBIA HOTLINE?
MACNELLY

Y'KNOW, BECAUSE THIS PLACE IS SUCH A HANGOUT FOR ALL OF YOU NEWSPAPER GUYS IT'S GOTTEN QUITE A REPUTATION.
IN FACT, IT'S BEING WRITTEN UP IN AN INTERNATIONAL PUBLICATION.
YOU MEAN THE MICHELIN GUIDE OR SOMETHING?
NO, THE GUINNESS BOOK OF WORLD RECORDS — UNDER "LOWEST TIPPING."
MACNELLY

I FINALLY FOUND A FITNESS BOOK WRITTEN BY A BIG STAR I CAN REALLY RELATE TO...
The Orson Welles Workout Book.
MACNELLY

A TIP FOR BACHELORS...
IF YOU DO YOUR WASH IN A PUBLIC LAUNDROMAT...
AVOID FESTIVE PAJAMAS.
MACNELLY

PERFESSER! YOU ARE DEVELOPING QUITE A BAY WINDOW THERE.
YEAH, I GUESS...
OH WELL...
EVERYONE SHOULD BE OUTSTANDING AT SOMETHING.

MMMF!
URRUPPH!
FOOM!
THE RECLINER IS OVER HERE.

DO YOU EVER CLEAN OUT THE INSIDE OF YOUR TRUCK?
OH YEAH...
I RUN IT THROUGH THE CAR WASH EVERY FEW MONTHS.
WITH THE DOORS OPEN.

THE COFFEE IS CERTAINLY MORE INTERESTING NOW THAT YOU'RE MAKING IT...
THANKS.... DO YOU WANT ANOTHER CUP?
SURE...
BUT THIS TIME HOLD THE FRUIT SALAD AND THE LITTLE BAMBOO UMBRELLA.
MACNELLY

YECCH!! THIS ★#@?!! COFFEE!!
WHAT'S THE MATTER? IT'S CINNAMON CAFÉ AU LAIT À LA MODE. IT'S DELICIOUS!!
– I KNOW.
COFFEE'S NOT SUPPOSED TO TASTE GOOD.
MACNELLY

WHEN WOULD YOU LIKE TO DINE, SIR?
DON'T WORRY ABOUT DINNER, BUMPKINS. I'LL FIX MY OWN.
VERY WELL, SIR.
THEN WILL YOU BE NEEDING ASSISTANCE WITH THE CAN OPENER?
MACNELLY

I DON'T SEE HOW YOU CAN GAG DOWN THAT COFFEE.
I LOVE IT!
COFFEE IS LIKE HAVING DESSERT AFTER BREAKFAST.
OF COURSE, IF YOU HAVE A CIGAR FOR BREAKFAST, ANYTHING TASTES GREAT.
MACNELLY

SHOULD WE COVER THE INTERNATIONAL CONVENTION OF ATTORNEYS GENERAL OF WEIRDLY SHAPED STATES?
HECK, NO!! I CAN'T IMAGINE ANYTHING MORE BORING.
IT'S IN BERMUDA.
ON THE OTHER HAND, WHO AM I TO STAND IN THE WAY OF THE PEOPLE'S RIGHT TO KNOW?
MACNELLY

WHAT'LL IT BE, PERFESSER?
GEE, I DON'T KNOW, ROZ...
IT'S BEEN SUCH A ROUGH DAY...
I GUESS I'LL HAVE WHAT THE GENTLEMAN ON THE FLOOR IS HAVING.
MACNELLY

THAT MUST BE MASTER SKYLER'S BUS NOW, SIR...
YUP... I MISSED THE LITTLE SQUIRT WHILE HE WAS OFF AT CAMP.
SCREE!!
SKYLER! HOW WAS..
CAMP?...
DELAYED STRESS SYNDROME, IF I'M NOT MISTAKEN...

WELL, SKYLER... TELL ME ABOUT SUMMER CAMP...
KNOWING YOU, I BET YOU CAME BACK WITH A TRUNKFUL OF PRIZES AND TROPHIES..
NAH.
BUT I DID GET THIS NEAT TATTOO...
MACNELLY

AH, THE FOURTH OF JULY!! THIS IS ONE OF THOSE DAYS THAT I REALLY FEEL LIKE A FREE MAN.
JUST BECAUSE YOU'VE GOT THE DAY OFF?
OFFICE
NO, BECAUSE THE GOVERNMENT HAS THE DAY OFF.
MACNELLY

I KNEW IT. I KNEW IT! IF I QUIT SMOKING, I'D GAIN WEIGHT.
COME ON, ROZ. YOU DON'T JUST PUT ON WEIGHT OVERNIGHT.
I DO.... IT HAPPENS EVERY TIME I'VE TRIED THIS METHOD.
SEE? I'VE ALREADY GAINED THREE POUNDS.
MACNELLY

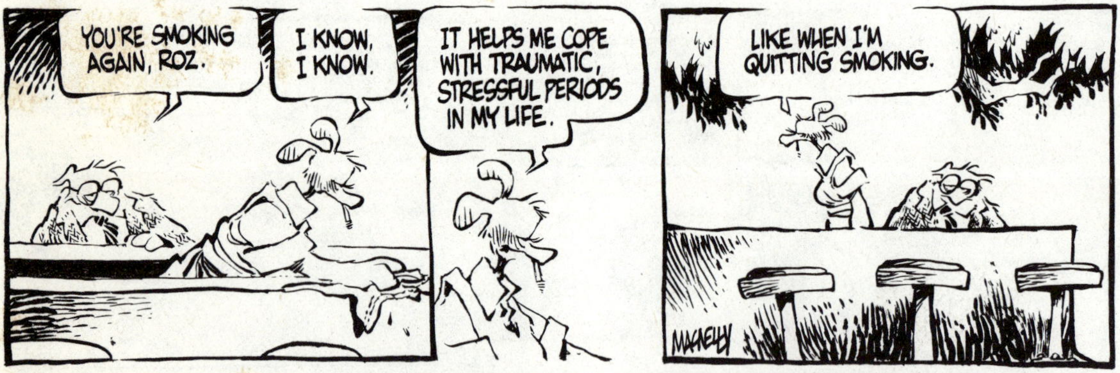
YOU'RE SMOKING AGAIN, ROZ.
I KNOW, I KNOW.
IT HELPS ME COPE WITH TRAUMATIC, STRESSFUL PERIODS IN MY LIFE.
LIKE WHEN I'M QUITTING SMOKING.
MACNELLY

ISN'T IT HARD ON YOUR BOOKS AND MAGAZINES THROWING THEM AROUND THE ROOM LIKE THIS?
I GUESS SO...
BUT IT PROTECTS MY FLOORS...
MACNELLY

PLAYING THE VIDEO GAMES AGAIN?
RIGHT, UNCLE COSMO.
DAGNABBIT!!
EEP BEEPA BEEP
BINKA BINK
GADS, THESE MACHINES ARE A HIDEOUS PLAGUE!!
OH NO!!
BINK! EEP! EEP EEP! GRONKA
POIT POIT
THESE INFERNAL BEEPING CONTRAPTIONS ARE ROTTING YOUR FRONTAL LOBES!!
DARN!!
EEP!
BEEP BINKA
BINKA
BEEP
YOUR BRAINS ARE TURNING TO MUSH!!
YOU'VE GOT TO THINK ABOUT YOUR FUTURE!
YOU'LL NEVER LEARN ANYTHING USEFUL FROM PLAYING THESE THINGS!!
VIDE
CENT
DAGNABBIT...
#?!!
KIDS...
BINKA BINKA BEEP
BEEP BEEP EEP EEP
EEP BEEP
MACNELLY

LISTEN TO THAT, SKYLER!!...
AIYE
IT'S THE MOURNFUL CALL OF THE LOON...
AYAHEEEEAYEEEEE
AIYEEEAHEEE
GEE, THAT'S SCARY...
I WONDER WHAT HE'S SAYING...
WELL, IT'S A CLASSIC, PRIMITIVE CALL OF THE WILD...
WE CAN ONLY GUESS AT WHAT IT MEANS...
ACTUALLY, IT'S A PRIMITIVE WAY OF SAYING, "MY BUTT IS FREEZING IN THIS @☆#? LAKE!!"
MACNELLY

SHOE
THE SENATOR IS THROWING A BIG BLACKTIE FUNDRAISER AT THE BARBISOL PLAZA...
EVERYONE'S GONNA BE THERE...NETWORKS, TIME, NEWSWEEK, THE TIMES, THE POST...
I GOT A SEAT FOR YOU AT THE SPECIAL PRESS TABLE.
GET DOWN THERE AND SEE WHAT YOU CAN DIG UP...
PARDON ME ... WHERE'S THE PRESS SITTING?
BARBISOL Plaza
—NEVER MIND.
MACNELLY

SHOE
BUGS ARE NO PROBLEM OUT HERE NOW THAT I HAVE ONE OF THOSE BUG ZAPPERS...
SEE, IT ATTRACTS THE BUGS TO THE LIGHT AND ZAPS THEM.
Z-ZAP
ZAZ
YUKKO.
ZAPARRRGH
DOESN'T THE NOISE GET TO YOU?..
ZAZT
OH, YOU GET USED TO IT...
IT'S JUST A QUICK CRACKLE OF ELECTRICITY..,
ZAP
IT'S NOT THE SOUND OF THE MACHINE THAT BOTHERS ME...
IT'S THE SCREAM OF THE MOSQUITOES.
ZAPAIYEEE!
ZZAPONCH!
ZAPARRRGH!!
MACNELLY

SHOE
THIS TIME HE'D BETTER NOT THROW THAT SUNDAY PAPER THROUGH MY WINDOW AGAIN...
THE PERFESSER HAS BEEN ON MY CASE ABOUT THE ACCURACY OF MY PAPER ROUTE DELIVERIES...
SO I'M MAKING THIS RUN REAL LOW—RIGHT DOWN ON THE DECK...
TARGET IN SIGHT... OOF...
OH, NO...
THIS TIME HE'S GONE TOO FAR!! RUN FOR IT!!
HE'S MIRVED HIS DELIVERY SYSTEM!!
MACNELLY

SHOE
13
When executing a particularly difficult bunker shot onto the green....
it's sometimes very helpful to have your caddy or partner hold the flagstick.
This enables you to judge the distance to the hole a little more accurately,...
and it helps you concentrate on this most tricky shot
without the distraction of a spectator looking over your shoulder.
Anyway, what he doesn't know won't hurt him.
GREAT SHOT!
13
MACNELLY

SHOE
GOOD MORNING.
HOLD IT, BUDDY...
LET'S SEE YOUR PASS.
BUT I'M PERFESSER COSMO FISHHAWK— I WORK HERE.
SORRY, YOU'LL HAVE TO SHOW ME SOME KIND OF IDENTIFICATION...
Treetops TATTLER Tribune
SURE...
YUP... YOU'RE HIM ALL RIGHT...
MACNELLY

SHOE
WHOA NOW!! CATCH THOSE TWO SPACE CADETS THERE..
I BELIEVE THOSE ARE SPECIMENS OF THE PUNK ROCK VARIETY...
WELL, THEY OUGHTA CRAWL BACK UNDER THEIR ROCK...
DO YOU THINK THEY COULD EVER GET A JOB LOOKING LIKE THAT?..
SURE... MAYBE IN THE MOVIES...
IF THEY EVER DO "WEST SIDE STORY" ON SATURN... HAR HAAAR!!
HA HAAA HAA HOHO!!
HOHOHOHO AHEE HAW HAR HAR
WILL YOU CLOWNS KNOCK IT OFF?
THOSE TWO HAPPEN TO BE REGULAR CUSTOMERS OF MINE! THEY DON'T CAUSE ANY TROUBLE, AND THEY ARE WELCOME IN MY RESTAURANT!!
IT'S A FREE COUNTRY!!
BESIDES, THEY SCARE OFF THE COCKROACHES...
MACNELLY

SHOE®
NO, SKYLER, YOU DON'T WANT TO TAKE UP GOLF, BELIEVE ME.
IT'S A SILLY GAME.
YOU WANDER AROUND TRYING TO HIT A LITTLE WHITE BALL WITH THIS RIDICULOUS DEVICE.
AND WHEN YOU FINALLY DO HIT THE BALL ...
YOU SPEND THE DAY SEARCHING FOR IT IN THE TALL GRASS...
NO, SKYLER, YOU NEED TO LEARN TENNIS—A MUCH MORE SENSIBLE PASTIME.
COME ON, I'LL GIVE YOU SOME POINTERS.
UH... DO YOU THINK I HIT IT THIS FAR?
MACNELLY

SHOE®
THE WONDERFUL THING ABOUT RUNNING FOR PRESIDENT IS THE OPPORTUNITY IT AFFORDS ME TO MEET SO MANY DIFFERENT FOLKS, AND MY EXPERIENCE HERE IN NEW HAMPSHIRE IS NO EXCEPTION.
OH BROTHER.
WHY, JUST THIS AFTERNOON I MET A LOCAL GENTLEMAN...
HE WAS JUST YOUR AVERAGE JOE... BUT, LIKE MANY OF THE PEOPLE I'VE MET HERE,
HE HAD AN IMPRESSIVE GRASP OF THE ISSUES.
IT'S AMAZING, BUT IT SEEMS LIKE EVERYONE IN THIS STATE THAT I'VE TALKED TO HAS BEEN - LIKE THIS GUY I SAW TODAY -
WELL-INFORMED, SMILING, EAGER TO EXCHANGE IDEAS AND INTENSELY INTERESTED IN OUR POLITICAL PROCESS.
THESE FOLKS IN NEW HAMPSHIRE ARE A GLOWING EXAMPLE TO ALL AMERICANS.
DID YOU GET THIS GUY'S NAME?
JOHN GLENN.
MACNELLY

SHOE®
FRIENDS, THIS MINISTRY IS IN TROUBLE TODAY...
SO, LET US PRAY:...O, LORD ABOVE, WHO HAS RAINED DOWN UPON US SO MANY WORLDLY GOODIES!!..
WE KNOW THAT YOU ARE IN TROUBLE TODAY...WE WANT YOU TO KNOW THAT WE STAND READY TO HELP—JUST AS YOU HAVE ALWAYS HELPED US HERE ON EARTH!!
WE KNOW THAT, UNLESS YOU RECEIVE MORE MONEY FROM US, YOU CAN'T STAY OVERHEAD WATCHING OVER US...
SO WE PLEDGE TODAY TO SEND YOU A DOLLAR OR TWO OR TEN THOUSAND—(WHATEVER WE CAN AFFORD TO SEND)...
SO THAT YOU MAY STAY ALOFT!!
AND CONTINUE YOUR GOOD WORKS..
GOOD GRIEF! THIS CLOWN IS PRAYING TO HIS SATELLITE!
MACNELLY

SHOE®
WE BELIEVE THAT WE ARE WELL POSITIONED IN OUR CAMPAIGN...
WE HAVE A GOOD RECORD OF SERVICE TO OUR CONSTITUENTS.
PRESS
—WE'RE GRATIFIED TO SEE SO MANY OF OUR MANY GOOD FRIENDS IN THE MEDIA HERE.
HOW COME HE KEEPS SAYING WE ALL THE TIME? —WHO IS WE?
THAT'S THE "ROYAL WE."
MACNELLY
IT'S CALLED THAT BECAUSE KINGS AND QUEENS THOUGHT SAYING I WAS UNDIGNIFIED.
BUT, IN THE CASE OF OUR ILLUSTRIOUS SENATOR FROM EAST VIRGINIA,...WHEN HE SAYS "WE", HE MEANS "WE."
HE'S GOT SO MANY DIFFERENT STANDS ON EACH ISSUE...
AND, IN CONFUSION —UH, CONCLUSION:
— HE'S TURNED INTO A ONE-MAN CROWD.

SHOE®
SO HOW WAS YOUR SUMMER, SKYLER?
OKAY, I GUESS.
BUT NOT OUTSTANDING.
I JUST DID THE USUAL STUFF —CAMP, TENNIS LESSONS, LITTLE LEAGUE,
HANGING AROUND THE POOL...
WHAT'D YOU DO, LENNY?
WELL, I DECIDED TO HAVE A DIVERSIFIED SUMMER.
EACH MORNING I SET OUT TO EXPERIENCE SOMETHING DIFFERENT.
THAT'S GREAT.
SO YOU HAD A WIDE VARIETY OF ACTIVITIES...
RIGHT...
I PLAYED ZAXXON, FROGGER,... DONKEY KONG, MS. PAC MAN,... DEFENDERS, GALAXIAN, ASTEROIDS, ATTACK OF THE KREEBLES, BLASTON, CRABPOT, MAH JONG WARRIOR, FLAK, KABOOM, MEAT LOAF RANGER, GROWLER, ZAPPA, CRUNCHBUG, GRONF, SNAKE MAN, TANK II, BLASFO, ROACHER, MELVIN MAN, GOON RAIDER, FLINGER...
MACNELLY

SHOE®
The first book I read this summer was Oliver Twist by Charles Dickens
It was pretty interesting, I guess,
but it was real thick and very slow going.
It took most of the summer to slog through Oliver Twist,
in contrast to my other book,
Teenage Beach Blanket Desire by La Torra Flambé,
which I read on the bus this morning...
MACNELLY

SHOE
IN THE GOOD OLD DAYS OF NEWSPAPERING YOUR TRUSTY TYPEWRITER WOULD HELP YOU EXPRESS YOURSELF...
EDITOR
YOU COULD POUND THE KEYS HARDER WHEN YOU WERE MAD...
PRESS
AND PLAY THAT UNDERWOOD LIKE A PIANO WHEN YOU FELT POETIC.
MOST IMPORTANT, THOUGH, WAS THE WAY YOU COULD BLOW OFF STEAM WHEN YOU MADE A MISTAKE...
TAPPA... TAPPA... TAPPA.. PATTA....
YOU COULD RIP OUT THE PAPER, CRUMPLE IT UP AND HEAVE IT ACROSS THE NEWSROOM.
PRESS
ZIP!
SOMEHOW IT MADE YOU FEEL A LOT BETTER WHEN YOU DID THAT...
PRESS
BUT TODAY, WITH THESE WORD PROCESSORS AND COMPUTERS,... WELL, IT JUST AIN'T THE SAME...
BUT IT'S STILL PRETTY SATISFYING.
EDITOR
MACNELLY

SHOE®
BOY, ARE WE PLAYING LOUSY FOOTBALL...
THERE'S NO ZIP, NO HUSTLE...
WHAT'S HAPPENED TO THE OL' Esprit de Corps?...
HERE SHE COMES NOW...
IT'S MARY LOU FENCEPOST, OUR HEAD CHEERLEADER...
IF ANYONE CAN FIRE UP THE TROOPS, MARY LOU CAN...
YOU CLOWNS BETTER START HUSTLING OUT THERE OR I START KICKING FACE!
A UNIQUE, YET ODDLY EFFECTIVE INSPIRATIONAL MESSAGE...
MACNELLY

Our Last Act

QUICK, SKYLER... HELP ME STRAIGHTEN UP THIS MESS. TODAY'S THE BIG DAY.
WHAT BIG DAY?
THE DAY THE CLEANING LADY COMES.
MACNELLY

THIS HEADLINE STINKS! THIS IS A FRONT-PAGE STORY — NOBODY WILL WANT TO READ IT WITH THIS BORING, WITLESS HEAD HERE...
LET'S THINK! IF THIS STORY RAN IN THE NEW YORK TIMES, WHAT WOULD YOU SEE OVER IT?
PAGE 47.
MACNELLY

LOOK, I KNOW I'M OLD. I EVEN LOOK OLD, BUT I'M THANKFUL FOR ONE THING...
I'M THANKFUL I'VE NEVER LOST MY MENTAL... UM... UH, MY MENTAL...
AGILITY.
RIGHT!!
MACNELLY

LET ME HAVE A BOX OF THOSE "El Skunkitos."
YES, SIR.
CIGARS
THAT'LL BE $23.50 – AND YOU'LL HAVE TO SIGN THIS.
WHAT IS IT?
ENVIRONMENTAL IMPACT STATEMENT...
MACNELLY

NOTHING LIKE A GOOD CIGAR AFTER DINNER.
AT THE END OF A HARD DAY...
IT'S NICE TO KNOW THERE'S SOMETHING THAT STINKS WORSE THAN YOU DO.
MACNELLY

SKYLER, TAKE OUT THE GARBAGE...
AW, DO I HAVE TO?
YES YOU DO,... IF YOU WANT TO GO OUTSIDE TODAY...
I SEE WHAT YOU MEAN...
MACNELLY

SKYLER, YOU BETTER GET DOWN HERE AND PICK UP YOUR UNCLE...
WELL, HE'S HAD AN INDUSTRIAL ACCIDENT.
HE OVERRESEARCHED HIS WINE-TASTING COLUMN.
ZZZ.
MACNELLY

SKYLER, YOUR FASTBALL HAS TO COME UP A LITTLE.
REALLY?
AND HOW DID YOU KNOW THAT WAS MY FASTBALL?
IT ONLY BOUNCED ONCE.
MACNELLY

WOULD YOU LIKE TO GO WILDERNESS CAMPING WITH ME, UNCLE COSMO?
SURE! —I'LL GET MY COOLER...
HOLD IT... THIS IS A SURVIVAL TRIP... YOU CAN'T TAKE A COOLER...
BUT WHAT'S THE USE OF SURVIVING IF YOU CAN'T CELEBRATE WITH A COLD ONE?...
MACNELLY.

DO YOU TAKE AMERICAN EXPRESS?
NO, SORRY...
ONLY MAJOR GAS CREDIT CARDS.
MACNELLY

I'M BORED.
WHAT?! ON A NICE SUMMER DAY LIKE THIS?!
COME WITH ME, LAD! WE'LL PUT ON SOME WADERS AND WE'LL GO DUMPSTER DIVING!!
♫
AND I THOUGHT THERE WAS NOTHING TO DO IN THIS TOWN...
MACNELLY

CRAK
AH, YES... THERE GOES MY MOST RELIABLE PITCH...
THE FLY OUT TO LENNY AT THIRD.
MACNELLY

MY NEW KNUCKLE BALL IS JUST THE PITCH I NEED TO TAKE THE STRAIN OFF MY ARM.
IT JUMPS AROUND A LOT, AND IT'S HARD TO CONTROL,...BUT IT COULD HELP PROLONG MY CAREER.
SPRONG!
OF COURSE, IT MAY SHORTEN HIS CAREER.

IF YOU WANT TO THROW THE SPITBALL, YOU'VE GOT TO USE A SLIPPERY SUBSTANCE, AND YOU HAVE TO HIDE IT ON YOU WHERE THE UMPIRE CAN'T...
YES, SIR?...
SEARCH ME FOR WHAT?

ATTA BOY, SKYLER! YOU'RE STARTIN' TO WEAR OUT THESE CLOWNS, MAN!...
HUH?... THEY'VE SCORED 14 RUNS THIS INNING...
I KNOW.
THEY'RE EXHAUSTED FROM RUNNING THE BASES...

THIS ARTIST WHO WRAPPED THOSE ISLANDS IN PINK PLASTIC HAS A REAL PROBLEM NOW ...
I MEAN, HOW WILL HE EVER TOP THAT?
WELL, HE COULD MAKE THE PERFESSER A NEW SET OF PAJAMAS.
MACNELLY

HEY, IT'S HOT IN HERE... WHAT'S THE MATTER WITH THE AIR CONDITIONING?
— IT'S ON, BUT YOU HAVE TO BE PATIENT... I'VE CONVERTED OUR OLD, INEFFICIENT SYSTEM TO A MORE ENVIRONMENTALLY RESPONSIBLE, RENEWABLE ALTERNATE ENERGY SOURCE.
SUCH AS?...
SOLAR AIR CONDITIONING.
MACNELLY

I'VE DECIDED THAT THE ONLY WAY TO QUIT SMOKING IS TO GO WILD TURKEY.
YOU MEAN COLD TURKEY.
LOOK, YOU QUIT SMOKING YOUR WAY, I'LL QUIT SMOKING MY WAY.
MACNELLY

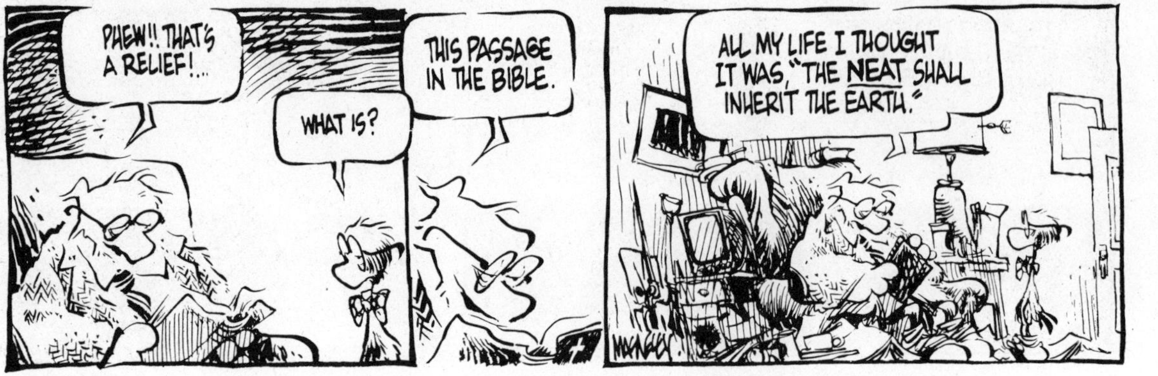
PHEW!! THAT'S A RELIEF!...
WHAT IS?
THIS PASSAGE IN THE BIBLE.
ALL MY LIFE I THOUGHT IT WAS, "THE NEAT SHALL INHERIT THE EARTH."

LET ME SAY HOW PROUD I AM TO RECEIVE THIS ENDORSEMENT TODAY.
MY CAMPAIGN FOR THE PRESIDENCY IS AN UP-HILL FIGHT, BUT IT'S MADE EASIER KNOWING THAT YOU ARE BEHIND ME.
ROAD GANGS FOR BELFRY
I REGRET THAT WE WON'T HAVE TIME FOR ANY PHOTO OPPORTUNITIES, HOWEVER.
PRESS

THESE CAMPAIGNS TAKE TIME. SURE, WE'RE BEHIND....BUT, WE'RE NOT DISCOURAGED. WE'RE BEING VERY PATIENT AND WORKING HARD.
OUR POLLS TELL US WE'RE ONLY 2 POINTS BEHIND DON'T KNOW....
AND WE'RE CHIPPING AWAY AT THE SUBSTANTIAL LEAD HELD BY DON'T CARE.

HOW DO YOU KNOW SO MUCH ABOUT ALL THE DIFFERENT WINES, PERFESSER?...
OH, I DON'T KNOW IT ALL.
I HAVE AN EXPERT I CONSULT FOR MY WINE-TASTING COLUMNS...
CURIOUSLY SURPRISING PERSPICACITY IN A WINE OF SUCH EXUBERANT PRECOCIOUSNESS...
MACNELLY

I FIXED YOUR OUTBOARD... I TOOK IT ALL APART AND IT SHOULD WORK FINE.
THANKS, IRV.
BUT HANG ON TO THIS BOX IN CASE OF EMERGENCY...
OKAY... WHAT'S IN IT?
THE PARTS THAT WERE LEFT OVER.
MACNELLY

WITH THIS RIDER MOWER I CAN DO THE LAWN FASTER....
AND HAVE MORE TIME LEFT TO LIE DOWN IN THE OL'...
FROMP
HAMMOCK.
MACNELLY

MR. SHOEMAKER CAN BE SO GRUFF AND MEAN—HE HAS NO SENSITIVITY AT ALL.
SOMETIMES I WONDER IF HE'S EVER HAD ANY TRAINING IN RUNNING A BUSINESS OR DEALING WITH PEOPLE...
OH YEAH... HE HAS HIS MASTER'S DEGREE...
FROM THE HANOI HILTON SCHOOL OF MANAGEMENT.
MAGNELLY

HOW LONG HAS IT BEEN SINCE YOU CLEANED UP AROUND HERE?...
AWRIGHT!! CUT OUT THE SNIDE REMARKS...
ANYWAY, WE'RE ALMOST THROUGH.
WE'RE GETTING TO THE BOTTOM OF THE PILE...
LINDBERGH MAKES IT!
MAGNELLY

MR. SHOEMAKER, WE THINK IT WOULD BE A GOOD IDEA IF WE GOT TOGETHER INFORMALLY ONCE IN A WHILE...
YOU KNOW,... THE WHOLE STAFF—MEETING IN A NICE SETTING WHERE WE COULD EXCHANGE THOUGHTS WITH MANAGEMENT—AWAY FROM THE OFFICE?
RIGHT.
KIND OF A WHINE AND CHEESE PARTY.
MAGNELLY

CAN YOU GUYS HOLD THE FORT WHILE I'M GONE?
SURE, CHIEF. WHAT'S THE PROBLEM?
BIG EXECUTIVE COMMITTEE MEETING. —IT'LL PROBABLY SHOOT THE REST OF THE DAY.
I BELIEVE WE HAVE A QUORUM....

MOST OF THE TIME CLUB SELECTION IS VERY IMPORTANT IN GOLF.
BUT IN SOME CASES IT DOESN'T MAKE ANY DIFFERENCE...

DID YOU SEE WHERE THAT WENT?...IS IT IN THE ROUGH?
SORT OF.
HOW FAR?
I'M NOT SURE.
BUT I HOPE THIS RIG HAS 4-WHEEL DRIVE.

OKAY, YOUR JOB AS SECURITY GUARD IS TO KEEP OUT ALL THE BUMS AND WEIRDOS, GOT IT?
YESSIR.
HOLD IT RIGHT THERE BUSTER!!
—EXCEPT FOR THE BUMS AND WEIRDOS WHO WORK HERE.
Treetops TATTLER Tribune
ONE FLIGHT UP
MACNELLY

The Stock Market rallied today in a broad advance
led by women's apparel stocks
I KNOW, I KNOW,...BUT I HAVEN'T HAD MUCH MAIL FROM THE FEMINISTS LATELY.
MACNELLY

DON'T YOU THINK YOU COULD USE A NEW TIRE?
SURE, BUT I NEVER REPLACE THEM ONE AT A TIME...
YOU ALWAYS GET A BETTER DEAL IF YOU WAIT 'TIL YOU NEED A COMPLETE SET.
OF COURSE IT SEEMS LIKE IT TAKES FOREVER FOR THAT LAST TIRE TO GIVE OUT...
MACNELLY

NOW LISTEN—WE'RE GONNA ORGANIZE THIS HOUSEHOLD OPERATION!
RIGHT HERE ON THE HALL TABLE WE'RE KEEPING A PAD AND PENCIL...
SO WE CAN WRITE DOWN THINGS TO GET AT THE STORE AS WE NEED THEM. —NOW.... WHAT DO WE NEED?
1. PAD
2. PENCIL
MACNELLY

COME ON, UNCLE COSMO, TIME TO GET UP!!
Z..
THE EARLY BIRD CATCHES THE WORM, YOU KNOW...
RIGHT, SKYLER...
BUT IF I WAIT ANOTHER HOUR OR SO I CAN HAVE SHREDDED WHEAT.
MACNELLY

WELL, HOW DID YOU LIKE THE CHILI?
VERY VERSATILE, ROZ...
VERSATILE?! WHAT DOES THAT MEAN?!!
WELL, IF YOU CAN'T EAT IT, YOU CAN ALWAYS USE IT TO UNCLOG YOUR DRAINS.
MACNELLY

I'M THINKING OF PUTTING SOME OF UNCLE COSMO'S OLD PHOTOS IN AN ALBUM FOR HIS BIRTHDAY—HE'S SUCH A SUCKER FOR NOSTALGIA.
IF YOU REALLY WANT TO MAKE HIM NOSTALGIC...
FIND A SNAPSHOT OF THE TOPS OF HIS FEET.
MACNELLY

OKAY, SON,... COVER YOUR LEFT EYE AND READ THE CHART.
E OPL STRMC
NOW THE RIGHT EYE.
E OPL STRMC
IT'S WORSE THAN I THOUGHT.
MACNELLY

IS THE PERFESSER OKAY?
I'M SURE HE'S FINE...
I JUST WORRY WHEN HE DOESN'T WAKE UP BY QUITTING TIME.
ZZZZ
MACNELLY

WHERE ARE YOUR GLASSES, SKYLER?
I'VE GOT A DATE WITH BERTHA CLUMP SO I REALLY DON'T WANT TO WEAR 'EM.
COME ON, SKYLER, SHE WON'T MIND— YOU LOOK JUST FINE WITH YOUR GLASSES ON...
MAYBE...
BUT BERTHA DOESN'T.

Y'KNOW, PERFESSER, AS YOU GET OLDER, YOU GET MORE DISTINGUISHED...
COME ON, MUFFY...
REALLY! YOU'RE AGING GRACE-FULLY, LIKE SOME OF THOSE OLDER MOVIE STARS...
YOU MEAN LIKE JIMMY STEWART, CARY GRANT,... GREG PECK.?..
NO. JABBA THE HUT...

WHAT'S IN THE BOX?
THE 26-VOLUME HISTORY OF MUSTARD.
BUT THAT'S THE LAST THING YOU NEED IN HERE— MORE BOOKS.
RIGHT. BUT I DO NEED SOME SHELVES.

HOW DO YOU LIKE MY PET FISH?...
HANDSOME, SKYLER... WHAT IS IT, A CARP?
ACTUALLY, IT'S A Glomioscisimum Garbanzolum Rex.
THAT'S STRANGE... MOM ALWAYS CALLED ME TOMMY.
MACNELLY

COME ON, BOY!! BALANCE THE BALL ON YOUR NOSE!!
HUH?
YOU COULD BE FAMOUS!! "Skyler and his Amazing Goldfish!!"
SHOW BIZ AIN'T MUCH IF YOU'RE A FISH...
I MEAN, WHAT'S LEFT AFTER YOU GET THAT GUEST SHOT ON JACQUES COUSTEAU?
MACNELLY

NO OFFENSE, MAC,..BUT WHY DO WE NEED A SECURITY GUARD AROUND HERE?
WELL, IT'S ALL THEM HIJACKINGS GOING ON...
WHAT? NOBODY'S EVER TRIED TO HIJACK A BUILDING...
NOT WHILE I'VE BEEN ON THE JOB.
MACNELLY

SHOE®
It's hard to believe as we sit at our space-age computer consoles and word processors...
just how much progress we've made in the field of communications in a relatively short time.
It wasn't so long ago when our ancestors could only communicate using very primitive means...
such as smoke signals, beating on drums, or just plain screaming.
Yes, we sure have come a long way....
BOOM! BOOM! BOOM
BOOM BOOM BOOM BOOM
sort of.
MACNELLY

SHOE®
WHOOOOSH
LOOK, UNCLE COSMO!! A HARRIER JUMP JET!!
A JUMP JET?...
YEAH. IT FLIES STRAIGHT AHEAD LIKE A REGULAR FIGHTER PLANE...
BUT IT CAN STOP IN MIDAIR INSTANTLY!!
...AND LAND VERTICALLY...
WOW...
THERE'S NOTHING IN THE WORLD THAT FLIES QUITE LIKE THE HARRIER...
WHOOOOSH
WONK
ALMOST NOTHING.
MACNELLY

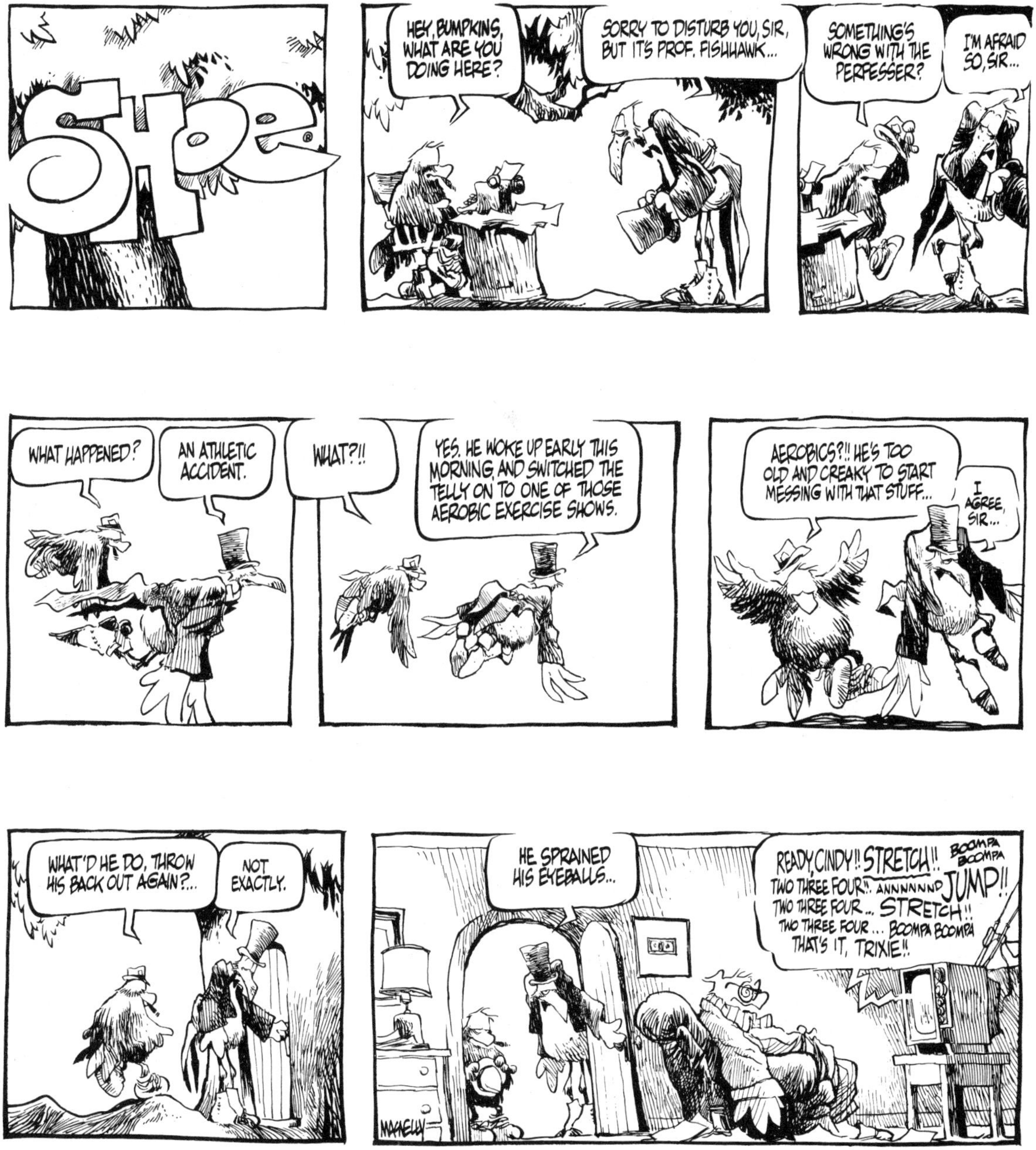
SHOE®
HEY, BUMPKINS, WHAT ARE YOU DOING HERE?
SORRY TO DISTURB YOU, SIR, BUT IT'S PROF. FISHHAWK...
SOMETHING'S WRONG WITH THE PERFESSER?
I'M AFRAID SO, SIR...
WHAT HAPPENED?
AN ATHLETIC ACCIDENT.
WHAT?!!
YES. HE WOKE UP EARLY THIS MORNING AND SWITCHED THE TELLY ON TO ONE OF THOSE AEROBIC EXERCISE SHOWS.
AEROBICS?!! HE'S TOO OLD AND CREAKY TO START MESSING WITH THAT STUFF...
I AGREE, SIR...
WHAT'D HE DO, THROW HIS BACK OUT AGAIN?...
NOT EXACTLY.
HE SPRAINED HIS EYEBALLS...
READY, CINDY!! STRETCH!! TWO THREE FOUR!! ANNNNNND JUMP!! TWO THREE FOUR... STRETCH!! TWO THREE FOUR... BOOMPA BOOMPA THAT'S IT, TRIXIE!!
BOOMPA BOOMPA
MACNELLY

SHOE
YEAH... SOMETIMES WE GET SORT OF ISOLATED IN THIS NEWSPAPER BUSINESS...
AND WE END UP WRITING ABOUT STUFF THAT DOESN'T MEAN SQUAT TO THE GUY ON THE STREET...
PERFESSER, I THINK YOU'VE LOST TOUCH WITH YOUR READERS...
YOU NEED TO GET OUT OF THE OFFICE AND DO SOME JOURNALISTIC LEGWORK...
LEGWORK...
SO I WANT YOU TO GO OUT THERE AND EXPLORE!! PROBE THE GRASSROOTS OF PUBLIC OPINION!!
TALK TO SOME PEOPLE AT THE BOTTOM OF THE SOCIO-ECONOMIC LADDER—FIND OUT WHAT THEY'RE THINKING.
OKAY.
COULD I HAVE YOUR ATTENTION?
NEWSROOM
MACNELLY

SHOE®
I'VE BUILT A NEW WORD-PROCESSING SYSTEM WITH ALL THE GLITCHES REMOVED...
SURE.
NO MORE WORRYING ABOUT LOSING YOUR STUFF SOMEPLACE IN THE MEMORY BANK — OR HAVING YOUR SCREEN JUS' GO BLANK — OR WAITING FOR THE PRINTOUT!!
NO, SIR! THIS LITTLE BEAUTY BYPASSES ALL THAT COMPLEX MICROCIRCUITRY, THE FLOPPY DISCS, THE BULKY PRINTERS, AND OTHER THIS AND THATS!!
THIS IS THE 21ST-CENTURY ANSWER TO TODAY'S AWKWARD, CUMBERSOME WORD PROCESSOR!
WITH MY NEW SYSTEM YOU CAN ACTUALLY COMPOSE RIGHT AT THE KEYBOARD AND GET AN INSTANT-ANEOUS PRINTOUT — WITH A FOOLPROOF MEMORY AND RETRIEVAL CAPABILITY... AND...
— THE GREATEST TECHNOLOGICAL BREAKTHROUGH OF ALL — IT SELLS FOR ONLY $119.50!!
IRVING, THIS IS INCREDIBLE!! WHAT'S THIS UNIT CALLED?...
GENTLEMEN, I GIVE YOU...
THE UNDERWOOD!!
MACNELLY

SHOE®
WOW! IT SURE IS WINDY!!
WELL IT COULD BE WORSE, SKYLER..
THE FOLKS DOWNSTATE PROBABLY HAVE SIX INCHES OF THE WHITE STUFF BY NOW.
REALLY?...
HOW CAN THAT BE?...
THERE ISN'T A CLOUD IN THE SKY.
WELL, THEY'RE IN A FUNNY WEATHER CORRIDOR...
DOWNWIND OF YOUR UNCLE'S DESK.
MACNELLY

SHOE®
SENATOR, WHAT IS YOUR STAND ON CAPITAL PUNISHMENT?...
YES, WELL, ...LET ME EXPLAIN MY POSITION ON THAT ISSUE BY OUTLINING MY REACTION TO THE RECENT SUPREME COURT RULING ON THE MATTER:
AS YOU KNOW, I AM COMPLETELY OPPOSED TO THE MINORITY OPINION IN THAT CASE...
AND TOTALLY AT ODDS WITH THE DISSENTING VIEW WHICH SUPPORTED UPHOLDING THE APPELLATE COURT'S ACTION...
STRIKING DOWN A CIRCUIT COURT RULING WHICH OVERTURNED A LOWER COURT DECISION
TO SUMMARILY FAUNCH THE BLARM OF MOMENTIOUS DIXIT IN THE STATE OF UTAH VS. JUDGE WAPNER...
WHICH, IN MY VIEW WAS THE RIGHT DECISION.
I KNOW THIS MAY BE AN UNPOPULAR STAND IN MANY QUARTERS,... BUT THERE IT IS...
THE MAN IS UTTERLY BRILLIANT...
MACNELLY

SHOE®
Twas the day we call Christmas,
Somewhere near the North Pole...
Not a reindeer was stirring
And Santa felt old.
If you took all the stockings he'd stuffed all that day,
They'd stretch clear from here to downtown Bombay.
He works all year long and worries 'bout others,
And takes care of them and their sisters and brothers.
But what about Santa,
Who has made a career
Of giving us Christmas
Year after year?
ZZZ
A kiss on his bald spot
Is all that he craves,
And he loves the pajamas
And this new aftershave.
MACNELLY

OKAY, SHOOT THE BALL...
COME ON, BOY! WHATSA MATTER?
I'M THINKING...
DO I PULL UP FOR A LONG JUMPER OR DANCE DOWN THE LANE FOR THE SLAMMA JAMMA?...
MACNELLY

NO, MA'AM, I NEVER HEARD OF A TANGENT, SINE OR COSINE...
I SHOULD?
WHOA, NOW!! YOU'RE PULLING MY LEG, RIGHT?
THERE'S NO SUCH THING AS SUMMER TRIGONOMETRY ...IS THERE?...
MACNELLY

BOY, SKYLER, I KNOW I CAN'T TAKE MRS. GRONK FOR A WHOLE YEAR...
SHE BELIEVES IN CORPORAL PUNISHMENT!!
NOTHING TO WORRY ABOUT, LENNY...
AFTER ANOTHER WEEK ON THIS BUS, WE'LL HAVE CALLOUSES ALL OVER OUR CORPORAL...
MACNELLY

THERE! I'VE GOT HIS FISHBOWL ALL FIXED UP JUST LIKE THE OCEAN.
HE'S GOT ROCKS, CORAL, SEAWEED, A SHIPWRECK.... WHAT MORE COULD A LITTLE FISH EVER WANT?
TRY PRIVACY.
MACNELLY

I'M THINKING OF ADDING A NEW ROOM ONTO THE ROOST HERE...
GEE, THAT'S GONNA COST A BUNCH.
NO SWEAT... I CAN SWING IT.
WHERE ARE YOU GONNA FIND THAT KIND OF MONEY?
I'LL GET YOU TO PAY YOUR BAR TAB...
MACNELLY

THERE'S NOTHING TO FEAR ABOUT GETTING OLD...
I MEAN, AGING IS JUST A STATE OF FLORIDA...
YOU MEAN "MIND."... "STATE OF MIND."
WHATEVER.
MACNELLY

LOOK, IF YOU DON'T LIKE WHAT I'VE WRITTEN, THROW IT OUT!!
WHAT?! THROW AWAY SOMETHING YOU'VE WRITTEN?
AND VIOLATE THE STATE TOXIC WASTE DISPOSAL CODES?!...
MACNELLY

LOOK, UNCLE COSMO!
I FINALLY TAUGHT HIM TO ROLL OVER AND PLAY DEAD.
TROUBLE IS, I CAN'T GET HIM TO QUIT.
MACNELLY

I NEED A NICE COMFORTABLE CHAIR FOR MY TV ROOM...
RIGHT THIS WAY.
SOMETHING LIKE THIS, PERHAPS?
LET ME GIVE IT A TRY OUT.
PERFECT.
MACNELLY

SO TELL ME ABOUT THIS NEW BOOK OF YOURS, DOCTOR...
WELL, IT'S BASED ON SOME FASCINATING RESEARCH WE HAVE BEEN CONDUCTING AT THE POLITICAL SCIENCE DEPARTMENT...
WE HAVE DISCOVERED FROM YEARS OF POLLING AND INTERVIEWS THAT 78 PERCENT OF ALL LEFTISTS ARE IN FACT RIGHT-HANDED.
THINGS A LITTLE SLOW AT THE OLD UNIVERSITY, HUH, PROFESSOR?...
MACNELLY

Once upon a time...
HEY!! WHAT THE HECK ARE YOU WRITING?
A WRAP-UP OF SENATOR BELFRY'S PRESS CONFERENCE.
MACNELLY

GIMME A LARGE PEPPERONI PIZZA...
YOU WANT THAT THIN AND CRUSTY,
OR THICK AND CHEWY?
JUST MAKE IT HOT AND MASSIVE.
MACNELLY

ARE YOU OVER 65, MR. FISHHAWK?...
YES.
GOOD. YOU'RE ELIGIBLE FOR A NEW FEDERAL HEALTH CARE ASSISTANCE PROGRAM...
MEDICANE.
MACNELLY

WHAT IS THIS?...
$4.75 FOR A DRINK?!
DON'T TELL ME— DESIGNER SCOTCH.
MACNELLY

PRODUCTIVITY REALLY STINKS AROUND HERE, YOU PEOPLE....
SO I'VE HIRED A MANAGEMENT CONSULTANT TO SEE IF HE CAN STRAIGHTEN OUT THIS SHOP.
READY, CONAN?...
MACNELLY

HERE IT IS, IRVING. THE OFFICE OF THE FUTURE.'
LOOKS A LOT LIKE THE OFFICE OF THE PAST...
THEY HAVE IMPROVED THE PAPERWEIGHTS THOUGH, I SEE...
MACNELLY

PERFESSER, I THINK I'VE FOUND THE ONLY TAX SHELTER FOR A GUY IN YOUR FINANCIAL SITUATION...
A REAL ESTATE DEAL?
SORT OF.... IT'S A BUNGALOW...
IN COSTA RICA.
MACNELLY.

HAS THE COMPUTER REVOLUTION CHANGED THE JUNK BUSINESS AT ALL, IRVING?
NOT REALLY.
THE JUNK'S THE SAME...
ONLY SMARTER.
MACNELLY.

PARDON ME, YOUNG LADY,... BUT THAT IS THE MOST EXOTIC HAIRDO I'VE EVER SEEN.
MENU
HOW DID YOU GET IT TO STAY THAT WAY?...
MACNELLY
I GOT IT CAUGHT IN THE BACKEND OF MY BLOWDRYER.

PARDON ME, SIR... BUT YOU'D BETTER WEAR THIS...
HUH? WHAT'S GOING ON HERE, BUMPKINS?...
AND GET DOWN BEHIND THE CHAIR.
WE HAVE TO DEFROST THE REFRIGERATOR.
MACNELLY

THIS IS ONE OF THOSE COMPUTER WORD PROCESSORS, SKYLER... I BOUGHT IT SO YOU COULD MESS AROUND WITH IT—AND MAYBE EVEN LEARN FROM IT...
IT WILL HELP YOUR SPELLING, IMPROVE YOUR VOCABULARY, YOUR GRAMMAR AND ALL THE BASIC LANGUAGE SKILLS...
GREAT! LET'S CHECK OUT THE INSTALLATION INSTRUCTIONS...
"1. First also may to put greatest tab A very fine and through the around slotting..."
MACNELLY

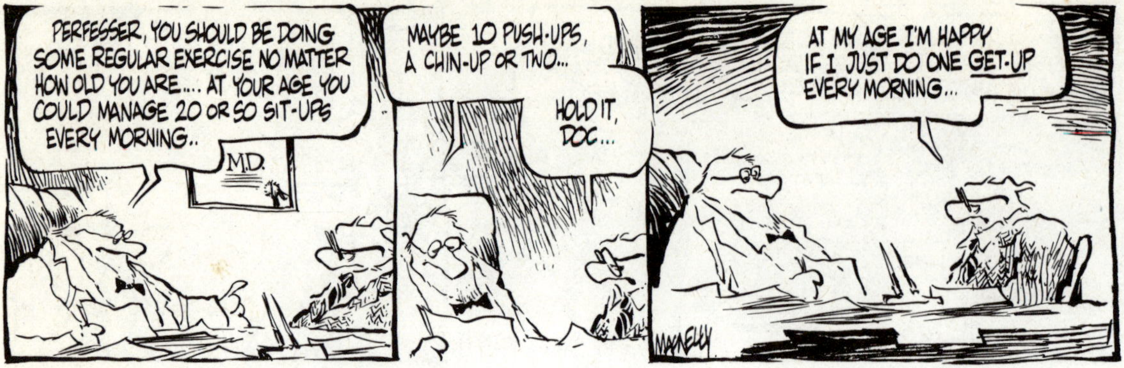
PERFESSER, YOU SHOULD BE DOING SOME REGULAR EXERCISE NO MATTER HOW OLD YOU ARE.... AT YOUR AGE YOU COULD MANAGE 20 OR SO SIT-UPS EVERY MORNING..
M.D.
MAYBE 10 PUSH-UPS, A CHIN-UP OR TWO...
HOLD IT, DOC...
AT MY AGE I'M HAPPY IF I JUST DO ONE GET-UP EVERY MORNING...
MACNELLY

inasmuch as manifest destiny and its subsequential policy foci were writ large in the American psyche vis à vis the precepts of the Monroe Doct
SHEE!!..
I KNOW BILINGUAL EDUCATION IS A HOT ITEM THESE DAYS...
BUT YOU'D THINK THEY'D WRITE AMERICAN HISTORY IN ENGLISH..
MACNELLY

WHAT SHALL I DO WITH THE DIRTY SOCKS, SIR?...
WELL, BUMPKINS,... WASHING THEM MIGHT BE NICE...
I WASN'T SURE, SIR...
THE POLICE ARE INTERESTED IN USING THEM FOR RIOT CONTROL...
MACNELLY

I'VE GOT AN IMPORTANT MEETING...
WITH THE INVESTMENT ADVISOR WHO MANAGES OUR PENSION FUND...
PUT THE BUNDLE ON Stumbling Prancer IN THE THIRD RACE.
TRACK→
MACNELLY

I'VE GOT A FOOLPROOF WAY WE CAN SHAVE AT LEAST TEN STROKES OFF OUR GAME...
HOW?
WE DON'T PLAY THE EIGHTEENTH.
MACNELLY

NOPE. TELEVISION WILL NEVER REPLACE US SPORTSWRITERS...
RIGHT. THERE'S NO SUBSTITUTE FOR OUR IN-DEPTH COVERAGE...
AND OUR THOUGHTFUL ANALYSIS AND LIVELY WRITING — TELEVISION CAN'T DO THAT...
BUT WE DO FIND IT USEFUL ON OCCASION.
BAR
SWUNG ON, STRIKE TWO COUNT IS ...TWO AND TWO—
MACNELLY

YOU WANT TO TALK TO MR. SHOEMAKER?.. JUST A MINUTE...
SORRY. I CAN'T REACH HIM...
MACNELLY

WONDER WHAT'S ON THE OL' SCHOOL LUNCH MENU FOR TODAY... LET'S SEE,... IT'S THURSDAY...
JUST WHAT I THOUGHT...
Cream of Wednesday.
BLIT
MACNELLY

SOMETHING'S WRONG WITH THIS COMPUTER...
—IT'S THE CARBURETOR.
THIS THING DOESN'T HAVE A CARBURETOR, IRVING...
EXACTLY.
MACNELLY

WE COULD SURE USE MOOSE ZINDERBLOCK ON THE DEFENSIVE LINE...
BUT I GUESS THE CHEERLEADING SQUAD NEEDS HIM MORE...
HE'S THE ONLY GUY IN SCHOOL WHO CAN HEFT MARY LOU FENCEPOST...
MACNELLY

IS HE ALWAYS THIS CRANKY?
HECK NO.
#! AND NAFF A BLIC, YOU NARB!!
SO ENJOY IT WHILE YOU CAN.
MACNELLY

DON'T YOU WORRY ABOUT THE CLOWNS FROM THE IRS AUDITING YOU?
NOPE... THEY'VE NEVER GIVEN ME ANY TROUBLE...
YOU SEE,... IF YOU KEEP ABSOLUTELY EVERYTHING — YOUR CHECK STUBS, BILLS, RECEIPTS, PAPERWORK, — ALL IN ONE PLACE...
THEY NEVER FIND A THING.
MACNELLY

NOW, WAIT A SEC. DON'T BASH YOUR COMPUTER WITH A BALLPEEN HAMMER!!
DO YOU HAVE THE OWNER'S MANUAL?
SURE.
BASH!
MACNELLY

MR. FISHHAWK, WE STILL HAVE SOME QUESTIONS ABOUT YOUR '82 RETURNS...
IRS
BUT I THOUGHT I ALREADY ANSWERED ALL THAT STUFF...
THAT'S THE PROBLEM.
YOU SEE, MR. FISHHAWK, WE AT INTERNAL REVENUE DO NOT CONSIDER "BECAUSE" A COMPLETE EXPLANATION.
IRS
MACNELLY

NOW WHAT'S THIS CLOWN RUNNING FOR?
I THOUGHT WE WERE FINISHED WITH ALL THE ELECTION CAMPAIGNS!!
THAT'S NOT A CANDIDATE, UNCLE COSMO...
THAT'S A GAME-SHOW HOST.
MACNELLY

HEY, WHO'S THE GUY WITH THE MINER'S HELMET AND THE PICK AND SHOVEL?..
HE'S DOING SOME WORK FOR ME...
YOU HIRED A COAL MINER?
NO...
A BOOKKEEPER.
MACNELLY

MR. FISHHAWK... ON THE MATTER OF YOUR BACK TAXES...
BUT I TOOK CARE OF THAT— RIGHT HERE ON MY RETURN...
IRS
MR. FISHHAWK,... SKETCHING IN A "BILL ME LATER" BOX DOES NOT EXACTLY TAKE CARE OF IT.
IRS
MACNELLY

THIS CEREAL IS AWFUL!!
BUT IT'S GOOD FOR YOU - IT'S HIGH IN NATURAL FIBER.
IF I WANTED NATURAL FIBER FOR BREAKFAST I'D FRY UP MY DOORMAT...
MACNELLY.

HOW DID YOU GET THIS JOB, RALPH?
EASY. I JUST TOLD'EM I HAD 16 YEARS EXPERIENCE IN SECURITY.
IS THAT TRUE?...
SURE.
'COURSE I WAS TALKIN' ABOUT SOCIAL SECURITY.
MACNELLY

JUST A FEW QUESTIONS FOR THIS INSURANCE FORM... DO YOU DRINK AT ALL?
WELL...
WOULD YOU SAY YOU HAVE AN OCCASIONAL SOCIAL DRINK?...
YEAH, THAT'S RIGHT.
THE REST ARE ALL OCCUPATIONAL.
MACNELLY

BOY, IT'S A GREAT FEELING TO FINALLY BE ON TOP OF YOUR WORK!!
AND THE VIEW IS ALWAYS GREAT FROM UP HERE.
MACNELLY.

I DON'T KNOW, SHOE... I FEEL SO DOWN... SO DEPRESSED...
LISTEN,... PROMISE ME YOU WON'T DO ANYTHING DRASTIC...
UNTIL YOU GET AHEAD ON YOUR COLUMNS.
MACNELLY

PERFESSER!! YOU LOOK TERRIBLE!
I DIDN'T GET A WINK OF SLEEP LAST NIGHT. THE NEIGHBORS HAD A ROWDY PARTY.
ON A WEEK NIGHT?! HOW INCONSIDERATE.
I'LL SAY...
I DIDN'T GET OUTTA THERE 'TIL AFTER 3.
MACNELLY

SKYLER!! WHERE ARE YOU?... YOU LEFT THE TV ON!!...
GOOD GRIEF!!... IT'S "INVASION OF THE BRAIN SUCKERS" —1957, I BELIEVE...
DOCTOR!... IT'S ONE OF THEM.... DOCTOR?...
YUKKO.
CLICK
HEY, I'M WATCHING THAT!!
MACNELLY

YOUR DIET IS ATROCIOUS!! NO NATURAL FIBER AT ALL!!
COME ON, ROZ,...I EAT PLENTY OF NATURAL FIBER EVERY DAY...
CHEWIN' YOUR FINGERNAILS DOESN'T COUNT.
MACNELLY

MR. SHOEMAKER,...DO YOU THINK THAT SOMEDAY I'LL BE RUNNING THE SOCIETY PAGE?
NOT HERE, MUFFY.
ALL WE GOT IN THIS TOWN IS A SOCIETY PARAGRAPH.
MACNELLY

HOW WOULD YOU LIKE TO WRITE A COMPREHENSIVE PIECE ABOUT WHAT'S WRONG WITH INDUSTRY IN AMERICA?...
GEE, I DON'T KNOW...
THAT WOULD MEAN A LOT OF RESEARCH WORK AND STUFF...
CAN'T YOU GET NAKAMURA TO DO IT?...
MACNELLY

YES KIDS, IT'S TIME FOR.... A GLOPPO BREAK!! WHAT?! YOU'RE OUT OF GLOPPO?!!
HURRY!! TELL YOUR MOM TO REMEMBER GLOPPO....
THE OFFICIAL JUNK FOOD OF THE 1984 OLYMPICS...
MACNELLY

GESUNDHEIT.
MACNELLY

HE JUST SITS THERE WITH HIS MOUTH OPEN – I CAN'T GET HIM TO RESPOND.
HAVE YOU TRIED CHANGING THE CHANNEL?
MACNELLY

WHAT A BEAUTIFUL LITTLE BABY...
OH, THANK YOU COSMO – HOW NICE OF YOU.
GEE, I DON'T KNOW, UNCLE COSMO...
THEY JUST AREN'T VERY INTERESTING AT THIS AGE.
MACNELLY

Y'KNOW, ROZ, YOU OUGHTA PACK UP THAT CHEESECAKE AND DONATE IT TO THE U.S. OLYMPIC TEAM...
REALLY?...
SURE. I CAN SEE IT NOW: "ROZ'S OWN CHEESECAKE...
THE OFFICIAL DISCUS OF THE 1984 OLYMPICS!"
MACNELLY

YOU KNOW IT'S GETTING BAD AROUND HERE...
WHEN THE ONLY CLEAN WORKING SPACE YOU CAN FIND IN YOUR OFFICE...
IS YOUR WASTEBASKET.
MACNELLY

HI! MY NAME IS SHOEMAKER,
MENU
AND I'LL BE YOUR CUSTOMER THIS EVENING.
VAP!
MENU
MACNELLY

YURI ANDROPOV WAS BURIED TODAY AFTER A MASSIVE STATE FUNERAL IN RED SQUARE.
IT WAS THE FIRST PUBLIC APPEARANCE IN SEVERAL WEEKS FOR THE SOVIET LEADER.
RENEWING SPECULATION ABOUT HIS HEALTH.
MACNELLY.

GENTLEMEN, I HAVE A CLEAR CONSCIENCE — I'M PROUD OF MY RECORD AND I HAVE NOTHING TO HIDE...
AND, GENTLEMEN, WHEN THE ROLL IS CALLED UP YONDER
WELL, I'LL ABSTAIN.
MACNELLY

WHAT'S THIS, IRVING?
I'M WRITING A COUNTRY SONG.
HOW WONDERFULLY POETIC!! THE WORKING MAN TAKING THE TIME TO EXPRESS HIMSELF IN MUSIC!! THE PRIMAL URGE TO CREATE LURKS WITHIN US ALL!!
RIGHT...
THAT AND THE PRIMAL URGE TO MAKE A WHOLE LOT OF EASY MONEY.
MACNELLY

WHAT DO WE HAVE FOR TOMORROW'S FRONT PAGE?
THIS STORY ON HOW GOVERNMENT TRIES TO MANAGE NEWS...
AND THE DANGERS IN HAVING A SMALL GROUP OF PEOPLE DECIDING WHAT THE NEWS WILL BE.
NAH, THAT'S NOT NEWS.
CRUMPLE
MACNELLY

IRV, YOU KNOW A CLEAN ENVIRONMENT BEGINS AT HOME.
IRVING'S JUNK
EASY FOR YOU TO SAY.
Home Sweet Home
MACNELLY

I STUDY ALL NIGHT AND GET A LOUSY C+ ... AND DUMB LENNY LUCKS OUT AN A!..
YOU MAY AS WELL GET USED TO IT, SKYLER...
LIFE ISN'T FAIR.
BUT THEN DEATH DOESN'T HAVE A VERY GOOD TRACK RECORD EITHER...
MACNELLY

YUP. FIRST THING EVERY MORNING I GET THE OLD CARDIOVASCULAR SYSTEM PUMPING IN HIGH GEAR...
AEROBIC DANCING?...
NOT EXACTLY...
I READ YOUR EDITORIAL PAGE.
MACNELLY

THIS STINKS.
YOU'RE ABSOLUTELY RIGHT, SHOE... IT'S A ROTTEN PIECE OF WRITING... YES, SIR.
THANKS VERY MUCH FOR YOUR INSIGHTS. I APPRECIATE YOUR INPUT — AS ALWAYS...
GROVELING MAY NOT BE VERY ATTRACTIVE, BUT IT WORKS...
MACNELLY

YOU MEAN WE DON'T HAVE A LEAD STORY FOR TOMORROW?— THERE'S NOTHING HAPPENING?
SORRY, THERE JUST ISN'T ANY NEWS TO PRINT.
WELL, I GUESS WE'LL JUST GO WITH OUR EMERGENCY FRONT PAGE.
NEWS SHORTAGE GRIPS NATION
MACNELLY

GIMMABIBABIBBAB DOLLABIBBOLLAH ABIDDADIBBIBBUB
GEE, I DIDN'T KNOW IRVING WAS SUCH A TALENTED AUCTIONEER...
HE'S NOT.
ADOLLABIBABIBEEAYEEEEEEEE.
I THINK THE MIKE SHORTED OUT ON HIS TONGUE.
MACNELLY

HERE'S YOUR PIZZA, SIR...
THANK YOU, MY GOOD MAN...
OH, YUKKO....
YOU'RE LUCKY, PAL!! IN SOME ANCIENT CULTURES THE BEARERS OF COLD PIZZA WERE EXECUTED!!
MACNELLY

THE PENTAGON JUST ANNOUNCED THAT THEY'LL ALLOW THE PRESS TO GO ON ANY FUTURE INVASIONS...
THAT'S GOOD NEWS.
NOT REALLY.
THEY WANT THE EDITORIAL WRITERS ON THE FIRST WAVE.

I'VE ALWAYS FOUND THAT ALCOHOL KEEPS ME LOOKING GOOD TO GUYS OF THE OPPOSITE SEX...
WHAT!? YOU MEAN YOU PUT ALCOHOL ON YOUR FACE?!
NO, DUMMY...
I PUT IT IN MY DATE.

YOU MUST REALLY BE BORED TO JUST SIT THERE AND WATCH THAT GARBAGE...
YEAH, MAYBE SO....
BUT IT'S BETTER THAN WATCHING THE STUFF ON TELEVISION.

DO YOU WANT TO GO TO COLLEGE, SKYLER?...
HECK NO.
I MEAN, SCHOOL IS OKAY, I GUESS...
BUT I DON'T SEE IT AS A CAREER...
MACNELLY

UNCLE COSMO! YOU'RE WEARING JEANS!!
YES, SKYLER, THERE ARE DESIGNER JEANS NOW —EVEN FOR US FULL-FIGURED GUYS...
WAIT... LEMME SEE WHICH DESIGNER...
"WIDE LOAD"?...
MACNELLY

THIS NEW POLL SAYS 83 PERCENT OF THOSE SURVEYED THOUGHT THE MEDIA WAS A BUNCH OF ARROGANT, POMPOUS KNOW-IT-ALLS...
WHO DID THEY ASK?
12,312 NEWSPAPER READERS...
AAAH... WHAT THE HECK DO THEY KNOW?
MACNELLY